The black water reached Bree's knees. Her night-gown swirled on its surface, and still, she took another step. In the distance, something was swimming toward her, just beneath the surface. It moved so sleekly, with such lightning speed, that it barely made a ripple in the water. Bree leaned forward. She wasn't frightened. Instead, she was filled with a calm curiosity, and an inexplicable sense of . . . longing. Yes, she wanted it to come for her. And there it was; she could almost reach out and touch it now. . . .

"What are you doing?" A harsh voice broke through the music and a hand grabbed her force-fully, dragging her out of the water.

POISON APPLE BOOKS

The Dead End by Mimi McCoy

This Totally Bites! by Ruth Ames

Miss Fortune by Brandi Dougherty

Now You See Me . . . by Jane B. Mason &
Sarah Hines Stephens

Midnight Howl by Clare Hutton

Her Evil Twin by Mimi McCoy

Curiosity Killed the Cat by Sierra Harimann

At First Bite by Ruth Ames

The Ghoul Next Door by Suzanne Nelson

The Ghost of Christmas Past by Catherine R. Daly

The Green-Eyed Monster by Lisa Fiedler

Dead in the Water by Suzanne Nelson

DEAD IN THE WATER

by Suzanne Nelson

SCHOLASTIC INC.

For Lilly, Kate, and Noah, who hold a magical
place in my heart

ISBN 978-0-545-54302-6

12 11 10 9 8 7 6 5 4 3   15 16 17 18 19/0

Printed in the U.S.A.   40
First printing, April 2014

CHAPTER ONE

Bree Danielsen studied the faded, wallet-size photo in her hands, and an icy shiver slinked up her spine. A pair of glacial blue eyes stared back at her from a face of a thousand wrinkles. A beaklike nose, a mouth set tightly in a razor-thin line, and a nest of grisly black hair finished off the effect. There was no doubt about it. Bree's Aunt Hedda looked like . . .

"A witch!" Bree shrieked, handing the photo to her best friend, Fiona, for inspection. Fiona glanced at the photo and nodded until her blond bangs bounced up and down on her forehead.

"Definitely," Fiona agreed. "Straight out of 'Hansel and Gretel.'"

Bree stuck her head around the doorway to her

room and yelled, "Fiona agrees with me, Mom! You are definitely sending me to live with a witch!"

She swung away from the door and collapsed onto her bed amid piles of clothes and open suitcases. Even though she'd known for at least a month now she was going to spend her summer in Washington, she'd put off packing until this afternoon, hoping that her parents would change their minds. She'd clung to the hope that this summer would be just like last year's and the year before: shopping at Bloomingdale's, morning bagels from the bodega on 90th and Broadway, afternoons sketching in Central Park, milk shakes with her friends at Serendipity 3. But this summer, her parents, who were both literature professors at Columbia University, were going to England to research a book that they were cowriting, and they were shipping her off to some town in Washington that was so small it didn't even show up on maps! And now her parents had called for the car service, and, according to her dad, they were leaving for JFK airport in exactly twenty minutes. "I am not going to survive this summer," she moaned.

"Of course you are, sweetie," a voice said. Bree lifted her head and saw her mom standing in the doorway, passport and carry-on in hand. Her mom offered her a reassuring smile. "And your great-aunt is not a witch. A bit cantankerous, maybe, but it's all for show. I'm sure you two will become fast friends."

"I've never even met her before. I can't believe you're sending me to live with a total stranger. Doesn't that qualify as bad parenting or something?"

"Your father's aunt is not a total stranger," her mom countered. "You met her once when you were a baby. You just don't remember."

"Because it was *twelve* years ago!" Bree sat up and glared at her mom, but her mom just laughed. "And do you know that it rains one hundred fifty days a year in Washington?" Bree persisted. "If my skin gets any paler, someone's going to come after me with garlic and a wooden stake."

Her mom smiled. "You'll be surprised how much the sun shines at Midnight Lake. And the mountains and trees are so beautiful."

Bree jabbed a finger toward her open window as a siren rang out in the distance. "Not more beautiful than Manhattan. Give me sirens and crazed cabbies over mountains any day."

She gave Fiona a pleading look, and Fiona cleared her throat and jumped in. "Mrs. Danielsen, are you sure Bree can't come with me to Long Beach Island for the summer? You know my mom and dad already said yes. There's plenty of room at the beach house."

"Please, Mom," Bree chimed in. "Fiona and I have never been apart for a whole summer before, and LBI would be so amazing! You can still change your mind. . . ."

Her mom held up her hand, shaking her head. "It's very sweet of your family to extend an invitation to Bree, Fiona. But we really feel that this trip will give Bree a healthy respite from the city. We want to give her a taste of a more bucolic lifestyle. Our hope is that she'll better herself with some transcendental excursions."

Fiona looked at Bree blankly. "Um, what did your mom just say?"

"She wants me to relax in the country for the summer." Bree rolled her eyes. She hated it when her mom spouted professor-speak to her friends. Talk about embarrassing. "I'm not sure about the transcendental thing."

"Look it up." Her mom laughed. She quickly kissed Bree on the forehead, then turned back to the door. "Time for you to finish getting ready. Don't forget to pack your summer reading list for school and your sketchbook. Just think of all the incredible things you'll find to draw at the lake. As Thoreau once said, 'The world is but a canvas for our imagination.'"

She disappeared down the hallway, and Fiona burst into a fit of giggles.

"My parents are weird," she said. "But yours are *definitely* weirder."

Bree tossed a pillow at Fiona's head. "You are *not* making me feel any better." She dumped the rest of her clothes haphazardly into her last suitcase, then sat on the bulging top so she could wrestle the zipper closed.

"Okay, seriously," Fiona said, handing Bree her iPad and MP3 player. "You're going to have a great summer. You'll text me from your beach; I'll call you from mine. We can send each other pics of cute boys basking in the sun. It'll be fine."

Bree looked at her doubtfully, but then forced a smile. "You're right," she said. She grabbed a hair clip from her dresser and twisted her mass of red curls into a tousled knot so it would be out of her way on the long flight. "It's all about attitude, anyway. As long as I have my sketchbook and my cell phone, I can deal with anything."

"Time to go," her dad announced, walking into her room. He glanced at her bed, his eyes widening. "Four suitcases? Isn't that a bit . . . excessive?"

"Hey, I can't take Manhattan with me, but I *am* taking its fashion. How else do you expect me to survive?"

Her dad grumbled something about needing a bigger car, loaded up the suitcases in his arms, and trudged away.

Bree took a deep breath, slipped her sketchbook into her carry-on next to her cell, and followed Fiona through the apartment and out the door of the brownstone. While her mom and dad climbed into the idling car, Bree hugged Fiona.

"I'll text hourly with tales of my pain and suffering," she promised.

"You better," Fiona said. "Don't let the wicked witch cook you for supper."

Bree giggled. "Not a chance. I'll leave a trail of bagel crumbs so I can find my way back home. See you soon!"

Bree waved through the rear window as the car veered away from the curb, then sank back into the seat as streets whizzed by in a blur, every block taking her farther and farther away from Fiona and her family's lovely little brownstone.

Once they reached JFK, there was a flurry of activity as they checked bags and went through security. Bree's plane was leaving before her parents', and before she knew it, she was already saying good-bye to them.

"Now, remember," her mom said. "Aunt Hedda will be waiting as soon as you get off the plane. She has special permission from the airline to meet you at the gate."

Bree nodded.

"You're going to have a fantastic summer," her dad chimed in, all too cheerily. "I used to love visiting Midnight Lake when I was a boy. It's like no place else on earth."

Bree smiled, but somehow that description didn't make her feel much better. She hugged them both and boarded the plane, wishing for at least the hundredth time that she was still back in their brownstone, listening to the thrilling hum of city life around her. As the plane thundered into the sky, she pressed her forehead to the window, keeping her eyes on the Manhattan skyline blazing pink in the setting sun. But slowly, the Empire State Building blurred into a gray smudge on the horizon, and the city faded into the dusk. Bree flopped back into her seat, already feeling sharps pangs of loneliness for Fiona, her parents, and her home. Maybe her parents were right. Maybe she would end up having a wonderful summer, after all. But right now, all she imagined was three long, dreary, rain-soaked summer months stretching out before her.

CHAPTER TWO

Bree stifled a yawn as she followed the flight attendant through the hallway that led to her arrival gate. She'd stayed awake for the entire six-hour flight, mostly drawing in her sketchbook. But now it was almost two A.M. New York time, and she could hardly keep her eyes open. All she could think about was a pillow and a soft, cozy bed.

"Your aunt should be waiting just through here." The flight attendant nodded kindly at Bree as they walked through the doorway into the open gate area.

Bree scanned the rows of chairs surrounding the check-in kiosk, but they were all empty. In fact, the handful of people passing by had just gotten off her own plane. Where was her aunt?

"Hmmm." The flight attendant gave Bree an encouraging smile. "Well, no need to worry. I'm sure she'll be here any minute now."

But the gate quickly emptied of people, and after a few minutes, the flight attendant cleared her throat awkwardly and checked her watch.

"I'm going to need to board my next flight in a few minutes," she said. "I'll have to take you to another waiting area and they can page your aunt from there. Okay?"

Bree nodded, her cheeks flaring, and followed the flight attendant through a series of hallways and "Authorized Personnel Only" doors until they reached a bleak room furnished with a folding table and a couple of benches and chairs. The flight attendant asked her to have a seat, and then, with some vague good-byes, slipped out the door. A few seconds later, the overhead intercom screeched to life.

"Attention, please. Would Ms. Hedda Danielsen please report to the Terminal B holding area for unclaimed minors? Again, Ms. Hedda Danielsen, please pick up Bree Danielsen in the Terminal B holding area."

Bree's shoulders shrank into themselves and she shook her head, glaring at the floor. Great. She'd been labeled an "unclaimed minor." This was like being handed the kids' menu at a restaurant, or getting kicked off an amusement park ride for not meeting the height requirements. Except, because the entire airport had just heard her name blared over the loudspeaker, this was *way* more humiliating.

Her stomach suddenly croaked loudly in protest, too, and Bree remembered that she hadn't eaten a real meal since she left New York. She dug through her carry-on for munchies, and managed to come up with a pathetically small bag of pretzels left over from her flight. She finished them off in record time, and then settled into her chair to watch the clock on the wall. It slowly ticked away the seconds, and then the minutes, until the black hands blurred before her eyes, lulling her to sleep.

She was lying on a white-sand beach beside a sparkling blue lake, the sun warming her face and a gentle breeze blowing her hair. She sat up on her beach towel to reach for her sunscreen when she felt a sudden sharp pain in her shoulder. It was a scaly black claw, dripping with rancid water and digging into her flesh. She struggled to break free and, through her terror, heard the beast calling to her in his thick, gurgling voice.

"Bree!" Again, louder. "Bree!"

She opened her eyes to see a gnarled, bony hand clamping down on her shoulder and a shadowy figure with wild, waist-length silver hair looming over her. Bree squinted in the glaring fluorescent lights as the figure took a step back, its features slowly crystalizing. Bree blinked with a mixture of relief and dread. The woman before her was much older than she'd been in Bree's photo. But there was no doubt about it. This was her great-aunt Hedda.

"There you are!" her gravelly voice belted out, sounding more like a growling bear than a human. "How on earth did you ever expect me to find you in here?"

Bree stared into those icy-blue eyes, her heart buckling. "But, you weren't at the —"

"Ack, never mind, never mind," Aunt Hedda said briskly. "We need to hurry home." She was already moving toward the door, so Bree gathered up her things quickly and followed. "It's a long drive, and my houseguests get a might ornery when they're hungry. They're bound to tear the house down if they're not fed soon."

"Houseguests?" Bree repeated, her head still fuzzy with sleep. "But I thought I was the only one staying . . ."

Her aunt shook her brambles of hair impatiently, as if Bree was missing something completely obvious. "Oh, you'll meet the others soon enough. They're a bit savage." She chuckled, a sound like pebbles grinding and popping under a car's wheels. Then she narrowed her eyes, looking Bree up and down. "But coming from that sordid city of yours, no doubt you're used to that. A summer here will do you good. I still don't know what your mom and dad were thinking, raising a child in that place, without any fresh air, starved for the natural world. It's a wonder you don't suffer from chronic asthma, with all that smog you inhale."

"There are twenty-four thousand trees in Central Park, Aunt Hedda," Bree retorted. "And I love living in the city." The response sprang out of her before she could stop it, and she immediately wished she could take it back, worrying that now she'd be in for a lecture about rudeness, too. But instead, her aunt surprised her.

"Well, good for you," her aunt said, the tiniest glimmer of respect shining in her eyes. "You're the one who has to live there, so I suppose it'd be a shame if you hated it. Maybe you'll learn to love Midnight Lake, too. . . . Your father always did, and so has the rest of the Danielsen family through the years." Aunt Hedda held the door open for Bree and motioned her through. "Come on, then."

Wearing a blinding red sweater-vest, muddy dungarees, and giant rubber wading boots, her aunt turned heads all over the terminal (and *not* in a good way). It was L.L. Bean meets Swamp People . . . a fashion horror show. They got the rest of Bree's bags quickly, though, and Bree breathed a sigh of relief when they reached the dimly lit parking lot and her aunt's rusted, faded blue truck.

The drive from Seattle to Midnight Lake was mostly silent and, for that, Bree was grateful. She was too exhausted for a ton of questions about her flight or her family, although she wasn't entirely convinced that Aunt Hedda would've asked them, anyway. She was just happy to look through the window, taking in the unfamiliar but beautiful skyline of downtown Seattle. In a brief rush of excitement, she asked her aunt if they could come back into the city over the summer to explore.

"Not if I can help it," her aunt responded, frowning at the windshield. "I'm not antisocial, mind you, just anti-city. Besides, you already know enough about city life. I promised your father I'd teach you a thing or two about our family's Norwegian roots while I'm still alive to do the teaching. Midnight Lake is almost more Norwegian than Norway itself."

Then her aunt cackled, and shortly after that, the lights of downtown Seattle disappeared as they drove into the mountains. Soon, a wall of trees sprang up, so dense it blocked out the moonlight above. Her aunt's high beams turned the trees lining the road a ghostly gray, but on either side of the car, there was nothing but thick blackness. Bree had never seen so much darkness before. Back home, the city glittered like one huge night-light. But here, the forest swallowed light hungrily, as if it was trying to hide some long-buried secret in the dark.

Bree shivered involuntarily, then reached for her cell phone to text Fiona. She wanted to tell her that her aunt looked even more like a Brothers Grimm witch in real life than she did in her photo. But when she checked her cell screen, she had no reception. Not one measly little bar.

Aunt Hedda gave her a side glance, and then snorted. "You won't get much use out of that thing out here. Most people at the lake don't even own one."

That did it. Bree's meager hopes for the summer shriveled into nothingness, and she spent the rest of the drive staring out the window until, at last, the truck slowed, turning down a winding gravel path.

"Here we are," her aunt said, just as the murky outline of a house took shape through the trees. "I'll give you a proper tour tomorrow morning." She cut the ignition and climbed out, switching on a flashlight and motioning to the truck bed. "My back turned sour last winter, so you'll have to bring your suitcases in yourself. I'll just be getting supper ready for my houseguests."

Before Bree could say anything, her aunt disappeared, leaving Bree alone in the darkness. She sat frozen in the car and was just starting to wonder how her aunt could possibly expect her to find her way to the house in the pitch-black when suddenly, a dim yellow light flickered to life in the house. It wasn't much, but it was just enough for Bree to make out a set of stairs alongside the house. She dragged the suitcases two by two up the stairs, finally getting all of them to the top landing. Then, out of breath, she pulled open the door to the screened porch and stepped inside. Suddenly, out of the deep shadows, appeared dozens of gleaming red eyes, all staring at her hungrily.

Bree screamed, and a second later Aunt Hedda flew through the front door and onto the porch with the force of a hurricane.

"Uff-da!" Aunt Hedda cried. "What do you think you're doing, scaring the poor things half to death like that?"

"What are they?" Bree shrieked, her gaze locked on the blinking red eyes.

She heard her aunt yank on a string overhead, and blinding light from two bare bulbs suddenly flooded the room. Her eyes refocused quickly, and as soon as they did, she stifled another scream. A dozen cages lined the wall, butting against the house, and they were filled with living, breathing creatures. A badger paced angrily in one of the larger cages, while a raccoon and a skunk crouched in smaller ones. A cage that nearly grazed the ceiling housed a screeching vulture, and another was full of rats bigger than any Bree had ever seen in her life. She took a tentative step backward, and the raccoon lunged at her, hissing and rattling its cage.

Bree gasped, backing against the screen door. It took every ounce of her self-control not to make a run for the truck to lock herself in.

But her aunt didn't seem the least bit fazed. In fact, she leaned over the cages, grazing her fingers along them affectionately. "Hush now, little ones," she crooned. "Your supper's coming. No need to bare teeth."

Bree could scarcely believe her eyes. Who was this madwoman her parents had shipped her off to for the summer, and what was she doing with these beasts in her house? Then a horrible idea dawned on her. "Are th-these . . ." she stammered "Are these your houseguests?"

Aunt Hedda nodded. "I'm sorry they gave you a shock," she grumbled. "Your father didn't tell me you had a delicate constitution. What a shame. Most people with Norwegian blood in them have nerves of steel." She tilted her head, studying Bree. "You're not going to faint, are you?"

"No," Bree said, a little too loudly. "I've never fainted in my life." Nerves of steel . . . whatever! Anyone would've been thrown off guard by this freak show of animals. Her aunt could at least have warned her beforehand. She took a deep breath, and then tried to ask as nonchalantly as possible, "So . . . what are they doing here?"

"Oh, I take in some of the local pests, as a favor to animal control," she said, dishing up a plate of what looked like cat food for the raccoon. "They really are a bother around the lake. But still, I feel sorry for them." She tossed some foul-smelling raw chicken legs into the vulture's cage, and then threw a mishmash of food scraps to the others. "Not a single one of them will live past Midsummer's Eve."

Bree peered into the rats' cage and felt a stab of pity. "They're dying? Are they sick or something?"

Aunt Hedda shrugged. "Just their time coming, that's all." She wiped her hands clean with a rag, eyeing Bree with a shrewd, unblinking gaze. "You still look peaky yourself, though. Best be off to bed with you. Your room's at the top of the stairs, and the bathroom's down the hall. The kitchen's just through the door, and there's a hot plate of dinner on the table for you."

With a wave of relief, Bree hurried toward the front door with her bags. Her aunt had already turned away, her focus back on the hissing, growling animals. But as Bree dragged the last of her bags through the door her aunt called out to her.

"Oh, and Bree. It's . . . good to have you here," she said haltingly, as if words of kindness were foreign to her. "Too much quiet does strange things to people."

No kidding, Bree thought. But she mustered up a smile and said with a sweetness that would've made her parents proud, "Thanks, Aunt Hedda. See you in the morning."

"Good night," her aunt mumbled gruffly.

Bree was too tired and creeped out to be hungry for the dinner Aunt Hedda had left out for her, so she went straight to her small, stark bedroom. She changed into her pajamas quickly and slid under the faded quilt on her bed, loneliness making her shiver even through the covers. As she drifted off to sleep, she tried to imagine herself at home, listening to the lovely lullaby of city traffic outside her window, tucked under her silky, soft duvet. But the shrill cries of the vulture on the porch made it impossible to think of anywhere else, and in a night of distorted dreams, the bird's shrieking blurred into shattering screams of terror.

CHAPTER THREE

Bree opened her eyes, and the first thing she saw was a hideous creature with fierce, slanting eyes and huge fangs staring in the window at her. She sucked in her breath, her stomach bottoming out with fear, and she buried herself under the covers, sure she could feel the hot breath of the beast on her neck. But after a minute went by and her head was still attached to her body, she peeked out from under the sheets. Then she threw back the covers and leaped out of bed, peering out the window, disgusted with herself. The "creature" definitely had huge fangs and glaring eyes, but they were made entirely of wood. It was the head of a beast, for sure, but it was carved into the wooden beam of her aunt's roof, which, as dismal fate would have it, sat just outside her bedroom window.

Was there anything about this place that was not straight from some campy horror film? Bree yanked the shade down, already grumpy and she'd only been awake for about two minutes. This did not bode well for the *rest* of her Monday. Not bothering to change out of her pajamas, she slid on the ballet flats she'd had on the night before, grabbed her cell phone, and tiptoed out of the room.

The house was still and silent, and her aunt's door was closed, so Bree took the chance to look around, something she'd been too tired to do last night. There was a simply furnished family room with a worn couch, frayed recliner, and ancient-looking television, and a kitchen even smaller than the one in Bree's brownstone, with a simple wooden table and chairs. There were a few bright spots in the rooms, mostly from the collage of plates that hung on the kitchen wall, each decorated with bright red-and-blue swirling patterns. But for the most part, the house looked as weathered and worn as Aunt Hedda herself. Bree sighed. So much for the charming vacation cottage she'd imagined. But maybe the lake would make up for what the house lacked. She guessed she had a few minutes to check it out before Aunt Hedda woke up. Her cell reception might be better outside, too. Maybe this time, she'd finally get through to Fiona. She so needed contact with another *normal* human being.

She hurried through the family room and out the door, practically running past the animals' cages (luckily, only the rats were awake to softly protest). She frowned at the drizzle coming down from the heavy clouds above and made her way down the outside stairs.

Once she was at the bottom, Bree glanced up to look properly at her aunt's house, something she hadn't been able to do in the dark the night before. Huge hemlock trees hugged the house on three sides, so thick and tall that only a scanty patchwork of the sky was visible. The house's exterior was a dark, chocolaty wood with a high, slanting roof that came to narrow peaks in several places, almost like steeples on a church. At the end of each of the wooden beams that held up the roof there was the carved head of a beast, just like the one she'd seen outside her window. Bree shuddered. Aunt Hedda's house was nearly as unwelcoming in daylight as it was at night.

She cocked her head, suddenly picking up on a sound she hadn't heard before: the gentle lapping of water, like tiny waves tripping over rocks. It had to be the lake. Bree's heart quickened. Maybe if she got closer to the water and away from all those trees she would have better luck with her cell. She followed the sound of the water away from the house and down a narrow dirt path bordered by dense grasses and shrubs. About thirty feet down the path, the grasses opened up onto a rough, rocky beach. A small, rickety pier sat farther down the beach, with a small rowboat tied to its base. But for the most part, the lakeshore was rugged and overgrown with reeds and cattails. There was no soft sand for tanning here, no boardwalks like at LBI, no snack shops. Just wilderness as far as she could see.

She held her cell phone up toward the sky and started walking along the edge of the shore, picking her way carefully over rocks until she came to a flat, dried-out lake bed. Here was the place! She was sure of it. She stepped out onto the cracked surface just as one precious bar appeared on her cell. Yes! She grinned, and speed-dialed Fiona, then listened for the delicious sound of ringing on the other end. Nothing. She hung up and redialed. Still . . . nothing.

She didn't plan on yelling, or stomping on the ground like some tantruming kindergartner. But she couldn't help it.

"What is wrong with you?" she shrieked, trying her best to strangle her cell phone into submission while she jumped up and down. And then it happened. The dried dirt under her feet cracked open, and she sank up to her ankles in heavy, sludgy mud. *Eeeuw*. Sure, she'd tried an invigorating mud mask with Fiona last winter (guaranteed to open pores and reduce blemishes). But this tarlike ooze looked way more primordial than spa-worthy.

She leaned forward and tried to pull her feet out, but they were stuck fast. She couldn't even manage to slip them out of her shoes. It was as if someone had poured cement over her legs. She yanked, pulled, pushed, and twisted until she broke into a sweat. But it was no use.

"I cannot believe this is happening to me!" she hollered, beating her fists on the ground. "Somebody get me out of here!"

"Hey!" a voice suddenly called back. "Quit scaring

the fish or there won't be any left from here to the Sound!"

Bree froze and looked around, but she didn't see anything except trees and water.

"Um . . . hello? Is there someone out there?" she called out. "I'm over here. I'm, er, stuck in the mud."

There was a rustling from the trees skirting the bank, and then a boy appeared carrying a fishing pole in one hand and a huge trout in the other. His jeans and T-shirt were faded and worn, the knees of his jeans ripped nearly from front to back. Prickles of inky hair shot from his head in all directions, giving new meaning to the words *bed head*. He looked just about as wild as everything else around here, but he was studying her so intently that Bree lost her breath, unable to look away. But then, suddenly, his expression shifted into nonchalance, and the spell was broken. An amused smile crept across his cheeks, giving Bree the sneaking suspicion that he'd been watching her struggle for quite a while before he spoke up.

"You must be Hedda Danielsen's niece," he said as he started toward her, his long legs clearing the rocks and logs underfoot with quick, nimble steps.

"I'm Quinby Stromhest. Quin, for short. Your name's Bree, right?"

She nodded, feeling her face flush. "How did you know that?"

He laughed, stopping at the edge of the bank to drop his pole and fish and pick up a large stick instead. "Midnight Lake is a small town. A person can't even sneeze in this town without about a hundred tissues getting waved in his face. Hedda's been talking about you coming for months."

"Really?" Bree asked, feeling a small wave of affection for her aunt. Well, it was a good sign that Hedda had been talking about her. It was nice that she'd been so excited about her coming.

"Sure," Quin nodded. "She warned us that you might need a little hand-holding, since the city had turned your good sense to mush. She was afraid you might get yourself lost in the woods, or some other kind of mess." He laughed. "Guess she was right, huh?"

"What?" Bree grumbled, the brief goodwill she'd felt toward her aunt turning to annoyance. "I can't believe she said that. This is *not* a mess. And I am *not* lost."

Quin squatted down on the bank, spinning the stick in his hands. "Well, you managed to get yourself stuck in the mudflats in your pajamas on your first day here, and no one who's from here would ever make that mistake." He stood up and picked up his catch and his pole. "But, if you don't want my help, that's fine. I've got plenty more fishing to do. Not that there's any fish left within a hundred-mile radius of your screaming." He started to walk away.

Oh, let him go, Bree thought. She didn't want help from someone so . . . so cocky, anyway! But another futile struggle with her encased feet told her that she *did* need his help, even if she didn't want it. "Wait!" she called out. "Would you just . . . wait?"

Quin froze mid-step and grinned. "Yes?"

"I could use your help." Bree took a deep breath, then mumbled, "Please."

Quin bowed theatrically. "Of course, milady." He retrieved his stick from the bank and crawled out to where she was stuck. "Okay," he said, wedging the stick into the hole so it was behind her heel. "I'm going to push with the stick and you're going to pull. Ready . . . go!"

Bree pulled with all her strength and felt her heel lifting slowly until it slid out of her shoe and, with a loud sucking sound, broke from the mud. The other foot came more quickly, and before she knew it, she was free, sitting breathless next to Quin.

"Thank you," she said.

"Sure. Oh, and, for future reference, there's no cell tower out here, so you might as well give up the fight."

"Wow, that's depressing. You could've at least broken it to me gently." She groaned, but he just smiled impishly. And when his eyes met hers, she saw that they were a swirling silver, like liquid metal. She'd never seen eyes that color before, and they might have been unsettling if they hadn't been so full of mischief, too.

He started to crawl back toward the bank, then added over his shoulder, "You better follow me."

"But . . . what about my shoes?" she cried, peering into the hole she'd made in the mud, where her shoes still lay buried in the muck.

"Hey, I got out all that mattered," Quin said.

"B-but those shoes are Italian leather," Bree stammered. "I babysat for a year to save for those!"

Quin shrugged. "They're not Italian leather anymore; they're lake sludge. But if you want them, you can get them." He flung his pole onto his shoulder.

"I've got to get going, but I'll see you around. Just try not to get stuck again. Next time, I might not be here to rescue you."

He raised one hand over his head in a wave, and then he was gone around a bend in the bank, disappearing as quickly as he'd come. Bree stared after him, feeling a mixture of curiosity about the strange boy and fury at his abandonment.

The fury eventually won out, because she managed to get her flats out of the mud, but only after lying down and practically sticking her head into the hole to retrieve them. Their bubble-gum pink leather was unrecognizable, and by the time she made it back to the house, she, too, was covered from head to toe in caked-on mud. Aunt Hedda saw her coming from the porch and met her in the driveway by the foot of the stairs.

"What on earth happened to you?" she said, hands on her hips, shaking her head in disapproval.

"I got stuck in the mudflats," she said.

"Well, you're not setting one foot inside the house like that." Her aunt turned on the hose attached to the side of the garage, and pointed it at Bree.

"What are you doing?" Bree squealed.

"Giving you a rinse," her aunt said. "I have to head into downtown and thought you might like to come along."

Bree brightened. Finally, she'd get reacquainted with real-life civilization. "Oh, I'd love to come with you," she said.

"But not until we clean you up," her aunt said firmly.

Bree cringed as Aunt Hedda hosed her down with the cold water, and then, after she'd passed inspection, she went inside for a proper shower to get the rest of the mud out of her hair. She dressed hurriedly and pulled her hair up with a clip, not wanting to waste a single minute she could be spending window-shopping. She envisioned a quaint but eclectic downtown with a charming Main Street lined with boutiques, restaurants, and a movie theater! And maybe, if it wasn't too much to ask for, a bagel shop? Her mouth was watering already, just thinking about it. After all, with what she'd been through in the last twenty-four hours, she deserved to have a little fun.

CHAPTER FOUR

Two hours and two blisters later, Bree started to fear that fun didn't exist at all in Midnight Lake. That morning, after politely turning down a breakfast of pickled herrings, Bree had watched her aunt visibly pale with disapproval and knew she had another strike against her. "You've never had *sursild* before?" Aunt Hedda had mumbled. "Don't your parents realize that teaching you about your heritage is important?"

"Well, I like bagels and lox," Bree offered, but that only made her aunt's frown deepen. Bree smiled gratefully when her aunt unearthed a box of muesli from the cupboard, but it didn't matter. Her aunt's mood had already soured. Her aunt asked her questions about school and friends, but the rest of their breakfast conversation was stilted and full of awkward silences.

So Bree couldn't have been more relieved when they left the house for the trip downtown. She'd put on a turquoise blue-and-white-striped summer dress she'd picked out with Fiona especially for this trip, and she felt good, ready to give a "wow" first impression to everyone they met. But when her aunt walked past her truck and started down a dirt trail toward the lake, Bree's excitement faltered.

"We're *walking* to town?" Bree asked as she followed her aunt down the muddy path skirting the lake.

"Of course!" Aunt Hedda said. "It's the fastest way to get anywhere on the lake, besides boat. Come on."

Her aunt plodded along steadily in her boots, unfazed by rocks and mud, but Bree struggled to keep up in her mule sandals, which skidded and slipped constantly. As they walked, Bree spotted houses rising up out of the trees, all looking much the same as her aunt's. They all had the same dark wood exteriors with the high roofs, and every single house was adorned with those creepy monster carvings. The farther they walked, the lower Bree's spirits sank. This wasn't a town as much as a teeny-tiny village of weirdness.

"You all right back there?" her aunt called occasionally over her shoulder.

"Definitely!" Bree called back cheerily. Her feet were killing her, but she wasn't about to admit that to her aunt. She was going to prove that the "citified" girl could hang with the toughest of them. But finally, when she had two raw, red blisters on her pinkie toes, she had to stop for a break.

Her aunt inspected Bree's feet, scoffing. "I figured you wouldn't make much headway in those flimsy things," she said. "Why didn't you wear your sneakers?"

"I — I didn't bring any," she said, blushing. Silly her. She'd thought she'd be spending most of her days barefoot on a soft, sandy beach. "I only brought these sandals and the flats I had on this morning."

"I suppose we'll have to take you shoe shopping first," Aunt Hedda said with finality. "Town's not far now, but I do have to make one stop first."

They rounded a bend in the trail and another house came into view. There was an elderly man sitting on the front porch in a wheelchair, and when he saw Aunt Hedda, he offered up a smile and a wave.

Aunt Hedda raised her hand, too. "Hello, Arvid!" she called out to him.

"Hedda!" The man's smile widened. "And this lovely young lady with you must be Bree!"

"Nice to meet you," Bree called, wondering if there was anyone in town who *didn't* already know who she was. She guessed not.

"Quinby!" Arvid called over his shoulder toward the house. "We have company!" Bree froze at that name, and sure enough, a minute later, Quin appeared on the porch next to Arvid. The second his eyes met Bree's, that mischievous grin reappeared on his face.

"Looks like you're going to go through a lot of shoes this summer," he said, nodding toward her muddy sandals.

"Very funny," Bree quipped, her face heating up.

"So you two already know each other then?" Arvid asked, looking from Bree to Quin. "Well, good. Maybe Quin could take you out on the boat one day for some fishing. Have you ever been fishing, Bree?"

"Um, no," she said. Fishing? If it involved slimy worms, there was no way she was going fishing.

"I don't know, Grandpa," Quin said. "She doesn't look like the fishing type."

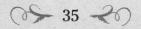

Bree read the challenge in his eyes, and before she could stop herself, she blurted, "Oh, I am! You can count me in!"

"Good!" Quin's eyes twinkled. "We'll go out later this week. You can gut the first one."

Bree swallowed thickly. Did he just say *gut*? Inwardly, she cringed. What had she just set herself up for? But outwardly, she kept her smile cool and confident to match Quin's.

"Well, we should be on our way," Aunt Hedda said. "But I made some salmon casserole this morning." She climbed up the rocks toward the porch with the tote bag she'd been carrying. "It's way more than we can eat, so I thought I'd drop some off."

"Well, now, you must have read my mind," Arvid said as Quin took the bag from Aunt Hedda. "I had a hankering for my favorite casserole today. You're a sweetheart."

Bree saw Hedda suddenly stiffen. "And you're a cad," her aunt retorted, turning back down the path while Arvid chuckled loudly.

"One of these days you'll let me court you, Hedda Danielsen," Arvid called after them. "I've waited fifty years, and I can wait a bit longer."

"Silly old fool," Hedda grumbled as they walked away.

"Is he a good friend?" Bree asked, glancing one last time over her shoulder to see Quin still standing on the porch, grinning at her.

"Oh, I suppose I'd call him that, if he wasn't such an awful tease," she said. "Arvid and his brother, Thomas, went to school with me, years ago. The three of us were fast friends, but then . . . well, things just changed is all." She cleared her throat. "He and Quin are all that's left of the Stromhest family, so they keep each other going. I swear, they live off scrambled eggs and the fish Quin catches. They're both too proud to admit to needing help in the kitchen, but I drop off food for them every now and then. Otherwise, the two of them would be skin and bones."

"What happened to Arvid's legs?" Bree asked.

"He lost them in a logging accident years ago, and since then, he carves the dragonheads you see on all the houses around here."

"Is that what those creatures are?" Bree asked.

Aunt Hedda nodded. "They're to ward off evil spirits. But they only offer protection for those inside a house. Step beyond the threshold and you're prey."

Bree giggled. She'd never heard of such a crazy superstition. But when she glanced at her aunt, there wasn't a trace of laughter on her face. In fact, her eyes were sober and disquieting. Bree broke her gaze, and just as she did, her aunt announced, "We're here. Welcome to Main Street."

Bree stopped and looked up, waiting for the quaint historical storefronts to materialize before her in a long line of charming pastel shades. But instead, she saw that by Main Street her aunt meant a gas station, a minuscule food mart, a bait-and-tackle shop, and a place called Anna's Bookstop Coffee Shop. Bree's stomach dropped to the tips of her blistered, muddied toes. There wasn't a bagel or boutique in sight.

"Let's get you some sneakers first," Aunt Hedda said, walking into the food mart.

"Sneakers in *here*?" Bree said, casting a doubtful glance at the mishmash of food and home goods crowding the shelves.

The lone cashier winked at Hedda, then smiled at Bree. "We're a catchall sort of place," she said. "The nearest mall's an hour away, so we carry some basics." She leaned forward and added in a conspiratorial voice. "We even have underwear, if you need it."

"No . . . thanks," Bree mumbled. She wasn't sure which was worse: underwear in the grocery store or pickled herring for breakfast. But she knew one thing: She could kiss her hopes for any normal sort of summer good-bye.

"Much better!" Aunt Hedda nodded in approval while Bree examined the blindingly white sneakers practically glowing on her feet.

She knew they didn't look "better." She already missed her cute sandals, which were tucked into a shopping bag along with the frozen waffles and cereal Aunt Hedda had bought for her. But, her new shoes certainly did *feel* much better on her feet.

"I just need to get a few quick things for my houseguests in here," Aunt Hedda said, motioning to the bait-and-tackle shop. "Why don't you run over to the Bookstop Coffee Shop? Anna has a daughter just about your age. I'm sure she'd love to meet you."

"Okay," Bree said, already liking the coffee shop's inviting windows full of books. The second she walked inside, the cozy smell of roasted coffee and cinnamon hit her nose. There was a barista counter on one side of the store with delicious-looking baked goods lined up along top. Two overstuffed arm-chairs sat near the counter, and a little girl who Bree guessed was about five was happily stacking blocks on the coffee table in between. The rest of the store was covered from floor to ceiling in dark-paneled shelves that were overflowing with books.

"Hi!" a friendly-looking woman said from behind the counter. A girl with white-blond hair and thick glasses sat on a high stool next to her, her face buried in a book. "How can I help you?"

"Oh, I just came in to look around," Bree said.

"Well, there's nothing better to do in a library," the woman said.

Bree blinked in surprise, and the woman nodded, smiling. "Yup, this is our town library, but it also triples as a coffee shop and Internet café. We're the only place that has Internet service in town." She nodded toward a desktop computer on a small folding table in the back, then she held out her hand. "I'm Anna, the little construction worker over there is Kari, and this bookworm" — she playfully elbowed the girl with the glasses — "is Nora."

Nora shook her head slightly, as if she was snapping out of a dream, and grinned widely at Bree. "Hi! Sorry, I didn't hear you come in."

"That's okay." She smiled back. "I'm Bree Danielsen, Hedda's grandniece."

"OMG!" Nora's mouth fell open, and then she squealed and catapulted off her stool, racing around the counter until she was nearly jumping up and down on Bree's toes. "You're from New York, aren't you!"

"Yes, I —" Bree started.

"I can't believe that I'm finally getting to meet someone from Manhattan," Nora gushed, grabbing Bree's hand and practically pushing her into one of the armchairs, accidentally knocking over Kari's tower along the way. Kari gave a loud shout of protest, but Nora just patted her head obliviously and plunked down in the other chair. "So where do you live? Soho, the Village, the Upper West Side? I *love* the city."

Bree smiled, waiting for Nora to take a breath so she could answer at least one of her questions. But Nora just kept chirping words madly, like a crazed bird.

"Is it true that real New Yorkers wear black more than any other color? And that there's a guy who sings in a cowboy hat and underwear in Times Square? And that somebody once saw a live chicken in a subway tunnel?"

Bree held up her hands and burst out laughing, surprising Nora into silence. "Wow," Bree said. "I've never heard anyone talk so fast in my life."

Nora's cheeks turned watermelon pink, and she blew out a breath. "Sorry, sometimes that happens when I get excited," she said. "It's just that ever since your aunt told us you were coming for the summer, I've been dying to talk to you."

"You sure know a lot about New York," Bree said. "Have you been there?"

Nora shook her head, then threw a slight glare in the direction of her mom. "No," she said emphatically. "I've only asked about a million times, though. I've never even been out of Washington State! I have to read about everything online. Mom's turning me into a backwoods recluse. I mean, look at me!" She motioned to her simple T-shirt and khakis. "*This* is not New York worthy!"

"You look fine," Bree said, trying to answer neutrally.

"Yeah, right." Nora stared at her over the top of her glasses. "If we're going to be friends, you better work on the honesty."

Bree giggled, delighted with Nora's no-nonsense

approach. "Okay, then," Bree said. "Honestly, you look like an ad for an outdoor sporting-goods store."

Nora threw her head back. "I told you, Mom!" she hollered, while Anna rolled her eyes from behind the counter. Then she grabbed Bree's hands. "You have to help me. I want to know everything about the city. I'll be your guinea pig, your fashion experiment, whatever."

Just then, Aunt Hedda walked into the store and, after saying hello to Anna, announced that they needed to be getting back to feed the houseguests.

"Okay," Bree said to her, and then turned back to Nora. "I don't know that much about fashion," she said, "but I packed way more clothes than I'll ever be able to fit into my aunt's dresser. Maybe you can look through them and see if you want to borrow anything. And I'll talk New York with you anytime."

"Tomorrow morning?" Nora said. "I can show you around the lake, too."

Bree nodded as she walked toward the door. "That would be great," she said, feeling excitement bubbling up inside her for the first time since she arrived. "I like to draw, and I'd love to find some cool things to sketch around here."

"Great!" Nora said. "I'll be by early to get you!"

Bree waved and stepped out onto the sidewalk with her aunt, happy to have something to look forward to. And the rest of her afternoon wasn't bad either. The sun finally peeked meekly through the clouds around five, and Bree took her sketchbook down to the lake to draw a few meandering ducks swimming in the water. She got so involved with her drawing that she lost track of time, and when her aunt's voice came sharp and loud from the house porch, Bree jumped. Aunt Hedda called her name a second time, and Bree looked up from her sketchbook to see shadows looming over the bank and the sun dipping behind the trees.

She stood up, stretched, and slowly made her way up the trail to the house. Her aunt was standing on the porch, studying the sky, her brow furrowed. "It's getting dark," she said. "There'll be a blood moon tonight." She glanced at Bree. "Come on in now. These aren't the nights to be outdoors."

What was her aunt talking about? Bree looked up at the sky with its hazy, purpling clouds, and thought it looked completely harmless. She opened her mouth to say so, but something in her aunt's tone made her think better of it. Instead, she went in quietly for dinner (macaroni and cheese from their trip to the store. Thank you, Aunt Hedda!). But later that night, as she slipped into bed, she noticed a faint red shadow slanting across her pillow, and she turned to see a huge crimson moon filling her window. Aunt Hedda's words came back to her, and a sudden, icy tremor skittered up her spine.

CHAPTER FIVE

The haunting melody came drifting in on the breeze, tiptoeing its way into her dreams. Notes so sweet and subtle they wove seamlessly into the whistling of wind through the trees, the lapping of waves on the lake. Bree opened her eyes and went to the window, peering out at the shadowy trees. Where was that music coming from? She'd never heard anything so beautiful. She longed to wrap herself up in the notes, to get closer to them. She followed the dips and rises of the song, out of the house and down the trail. Her feet carried her forward in a way that she somehow knew was impossible to stop, and even when she stepped into the cool lake water, her feet didn't slow.

The black water reached her knees. Her night-gown swirled on its surface, and still, she took another step. In the distance, something was swimming toward her just beneath the surface. It moved so sleekly, with such lightning speed, that it barely made a ripple in the water. Bree leaned forward. She wasn't frightened. Instead, she was filled with a calm curiosity, and an inexplicable sense of . . . longing. Yes, she wanted it to come for her. And there it was; she could almost reach out and touch it now. . . .

"What are you doing?" A harsh voice broke through the music and a hand grabbed her forcefully, dragging her out of the water. The notes suddenly fell silent, scattering on the wind, leaving Bree blinking in confusion.

Aunt Hedda's face was inches from hers, her eyes dark with fury and . . . maybe a little fear? "Come back inside right now," she snapped, keeping a firm hand on Bree's arm as she led her hurriedly toward the house. "You have no business being down by the lake in the middle of the night. Do you hear me?"

Bree shook her head, trying to process what was happening. Her head had a heavy, fuzzy weight to it, as if she'd just woken from a dream. Only, she hadn't been dreaming. "I s-saw s-something swimming toward me in the water," she stammered. She glanced back over her shoulder at the lake. It glittered red under the blood moon. The surface was as smooth as glass, as if nothing in it had ever moved at all. "And I heard music on the lake. It was so beautiful."

Her aunt stopped mid-stride and whirled to face her. She studied Bree's face with her shrewd eyes, until Bree dropped her own to the ground, embarrassed. "You're talking nonsense," Aunt Hedda said, leading her past the houseguests rattling in their cages and back through the house to her bedroom. "I didn't hear a thing."

But something in her aunt's tone had shifted, and Bree had the uneasy sensation that she'd just caught her aunt in some kind of lie. Did her aunt know where the music was coming from? Had her aunt heard it, too? And if she had, why wouldn't she just say so?

Aunt Hedda folded back Bree's quilt and motioned for her to climb into bed. "No doubt your mind's playing tricks on you," she said. "Being up in the midnight hours will do that." She gave Bree's shoulder an awkward pat. "Get some rest, and for goodness' sake, no more sleepwalking expeditions, unless you want an early grave."

"What?" Bree said. What an awful thing to say!

Her aunt froze, then shook her head. "I meant, unless you want to put *me* in an early grave."

"But I wasn't —" Bree started, but a warning look from her aunt made her snap her mouth shut again. She hadn't been sleepwalking, had she? She remembered everything so vividly. Still, she'd had the strangest sensation down at the lake, as if something outside herself was controlling her movements. But it hadn't scared her like it probably should have; it had felt wonderfully safe, almost pleasant, even.

Her aunt tucked the quilt under Bree's chin and switched off the bedside lamp. She straightened and went to the window, staring out into the darkness for so long that Bree wondered if she'd forgotten that Bree was in the room.

"So it's beginning," her aunt whispered.

"What did you say?" Bree asked, starting to sit up.

"I *said* . . . good night," came her aunt's brisk retort. She pulled down the blinds and clicked the door shut, leaving Bree alone in the darkness.

What is beginning? Bree wondered. And why was her aunt trying to hide it from her, whatever it was? With the stream of thoughts running through her mind, sleep was a long time coming. At last, her eyes finally fluttered closed, but the song from the lake remained in her head, replaying its melody over and over.

Bree woke up with the song on her lips, just as clear in her memory as it had been the night before. Golden sunlight needled its way around the edges of her blinds, and when she peeked out the window, she saw a brilliant blue sky trimmed with marshmallow clouds. She tossed on some clothes and, relieved to discover that Aunt Hedda was still sound asleep and wouldn't have a chance to forbid it, she rushed outside. She hurried toward the lake, determined to find out where last night's music had come from. Or, if she couldn't find that out, then maybe at least she'd be able to figure out what she'd seen in the water.

She crested the last little hill to the rocky beach and stopped short with a gasp. Something huge was lying on the beach, something with pale pink flesh covered in layers of algae, water lilies, and reeds. Bree took a few steps back, fighting the urge to run. But then she saw it — a hand nearly camouflaged by all the tangled grasses. A human hand.

Bree tiptoed closer, and a shock of wet black hair among the lily pads became visible.

"Quin?" Bree whispered, her heart jolting into her throat. In seconds, she was kneeling next to him. "Oh my god, Quin! Are you okay? Can you hear me?"

He didn't make a sound, and lay so still Bree wondered if he was even breathing. And then a horrible thought came to her. What if he'd drowned? What if he was . . . dead?

She shot up from the ground and stumbled frantically up the trail. She screamed so loudly for her aunt that by the time the house came into view, Aunt Hedda was already hurrying down the trail in her robe, her face pale with worry.

"What's happened?" she said.

"Quin's on th-the b-beach!" Bree stuttered. "I think he's hurt, or maybe worse."

And that was all it took. Hedda was already running toward the lake. "Go to the house and get some blankets and towels out of the closet by the front door. And there's a packet of smelling salts taped to the inside of the medicine cabinet in the bathroom. Be quick now!"

Bree never thought she could move so fast, but she was back on the beach in record time, out of breath, but with everything Aunt Hedda had asked for. Her aunt pulled a blanket over Quin first, and then waved the smelling salts under his nose, patting his cheek and calling his name loudly all at the same time. After a few terrifying seconds of uncertainty, Quin coughed and sputtered, and then struggled to lift his head.

"What?" he said weakly, rubbing his head as he looked around blankly. "Where . . . ?"

"Shh," Aunt Hedda said, untangling him from the lake grasses and helping him to his feet. "It's all right. Let's get you warmed up in the house."

She wrapped all the towels and blankets around him and then breezed right past Bree as if she wasn't even there, starting up the trail with Quin leaning heavily on Hedda for support. Quin didn't seem to notice Bree was there either, or if he did, he wasn't showing it. She followed close behind them, hoping to hear some sort of explanation of what had happened. But when they reached the house, Hedda told Bree curtly to wait in the kitchen, then hurried Quin to the back guest bedroom and shut the door, leaving Bree stunned and confused.

Bree waited restlessly, slinking into the hallway and straining to make sense of the rising and falling of the muffled voices behind the door. Finally, just about the time she'd made up her mind to bust into the room and demand to know what was going on, her aunt opened the door, nearly slamming into her.

Her aunt raised a stern eyebrow. "I told you to wait in the kitchen."

"What happened?" Bree asked, ignoring the reprimand.

"Just went out night fishing and fell off the boat, foolish boy." Her aunt waved a dismissive hand in the air. "He's lucky he didn't drown."

"Night fishing?" Bree echoed in disbelief. "Will he be all right?"

"Absolutely," Aunt Hedda said matter-of-factly, heading for the kitchen. "Just as soon as I get some breakfast in him." But she wouldn't meet Bree's eyes, and Bree had the feeling she wasn't getting the whole story.

"Why don't you go get ready for your morning with Nora while I take care of Quin?" her aunt said. "She'll probably be here soon."

Oh, great . . . she'd forgotten all about that. She'd been looking forward to hanging out with Nora today, but that was before everything had happened with Quin. Now, all she wanted to do was stay home to find out what was really going on. "You know, I changed my mind. I don't feel like going anymore."

Her aunt frowned. "Well, you're certainly not moping around here all day. Quin will perk up after a nap, and you don't want to disappoint Nora."

Bree had the distinct impression that her aunt wanted to get rid of her, and that she wouldn't win a battle over it, even if she tried. So she reluctantly headed down the hallway toward her room to get her sketchbook and bathing suit. But when she passed the guest bedroom, she found the door open and Quin staring at her from the bed, wide awake.

"So," Bree said with a tentative smile, "you didn't want to wait for me to go fishing with you, huh? I think I'm a little insulted by that."

She waited for Quin to smile, but he didn't. "You should be glad I didn't bring you along," he said. "Otherwise, you might've gotten hurt, too."

She was surprised by how darkly he said it, without a trace of teasing on his face, and her smile wavered. "Hey, give me some credit," she said, feeling a little defensive. "I *do* know how to swim, you know."

"That wouldn't have mattered much," he said sarcastically. "Trust me."

Bree stared at him in confusion. What was wrong with him? He was nothing like the grinning, teasing boy she'd met yesterday. This morning, he seemed so indifferent, almost mean. "Well," she tried again, "at least nothing really bad happened to you."

His sudden, bitter snarl of laughter made her take a step back from the doorway. "Nothing bad. Yeah . . . right." His voice trailed off and he turned away from her to face the wall. "You know, I'm pretty wiped, so you should probably go."

Bree nodded, suddenly feeling embarrassed that she'd even tried to talk to him. Clearly, he didn't want to be around her. "Okay," she said quietly. "I'll see you later."

He didn't answer, but she didn't have time to think too much about it, because just then the doorbell rang and her aunt called out, "That's Nora for you, Bree!"

She ran to her room, grabbed her sketchbook, suit, and towel, and was about to head for the door, but couldn't help pausing outside the kitchen when she heard her aunt talking in hushed tones on the phone.

"No, no, Arvid, I'm sure it's not that," she was saying. "I saw the blood moon last night, too. I remember the signs all too well." She sighed heavily. "No need to worry. You know it can skip generations sometimes. I'm sure he doesn't have the —"

She froze, catching sight of Bree, then cleared her throat. "I have to go, Arvid. We'll talk more later." She hung up the phone, and then smiled at Bree. And that's when Bree knew that something strange was definitely going on. That was the first smile she'd seen on her aunt's face since she arrived, and it was as unnatural on her as Quin's anger was on him.

"Go on with you, then," her aunt said, still smiling with feigned cheerfulness. "You and Nora enjoy yourselves, and I'll see you back here later."

Knowing that she wasn't going to get any more answers from Aunt Hedda or Quin, Bree gave up the fight. But as she walked to the door with a million questions racing through her mind, she looked back at Quin's room. And one question suddenly loomed larger in her mind than any of the rest: What had she done to get on Quin's bad side, and how could she possibly fix it?

"The swimming hole is just up ahead," Nora said as she dipped the oars smoothly into the water at a speed Bree couldn't possibly match. Bree had helped row for the first half hour, but her arms weren't used to it, and eventually she'd given up, realizing that the boat actually went faster if Nora rowed by herself. Once she wasn't busy rowing, she had a chance to take in the emerald-green mountains surrounding the lake, the lovely rugged shorelines, and all the wildlife, trees, and plants that Nora pointed out along the way.

"Wait until you see this place!" Nora said now. "There's a great blue heron nesting in the cove, and last week while I was swimming, a fox took a drink from the bank, right in front of me. He didn't even care that I was there. I bet we'll find some great animals for you to sketch."

"As if you didn't already find me a ton," Bree teased. She flipped through her sketchbook. "I've already filled five pages this morning!"

Nora grinned sheepishly. "I told you I knew a lot about the lake." Then she ducked her head hesitantly. "You're not getting bored, are you?"

"Are you kidding?" Bree laughed. "I didn't even know there was an animal called a serval until today! The most interesting animal I've ever sketched in real life is the polar bear at the Central Park Zoo. So, no, I'm not bored."

"Good," Nora said. "My mom says I'd make more friends if I actually stopped talking long enough for them to introduce themselves. But I always say, 'If they want to introduce themselves, then they should just interrupt me!'"

Bree giggled, loving the quirkiness of Nora's sense of humor. When they'd first started out in the boat, all Bree had been able to think about was what had happened this morning with Quin. But Nora's nonstop questions about New York had finally broken the spell. Her enthusiasm was contagious, and soon Bree was smiling and chatting easily with Nora, sharing all of her favorite stories about the city, glad to have an appreciative ear. And Nora really did make looking at animals fun.

"Here we are!" Nora announced now, steering the boat into a peaceful little cove and then jumping out to run the boat onto the beach. She stripped off her T-shirt to reveal her bathing suit and ran back toward the water, whooping and hollering.

Bree laughed and stripped down to her suit, too, but when she got to the water's edge, she hesitated, an involuntary shiver running through her as the memory of Quin lying on the beach flashed before her eyes.

Nora walked back to her. "What's the matter?"

"Nothing," Bree said, giving a little shrug. "The water just creeped me out for a minute, I guess."

"Oh," Nora said. "You've probably never been swimming in a lake before, huh? The bottom's a little slimy at first, but you'll get used to it. . . ."

"No, it's not that," Bree said. "It's just . . . well, Quin almost drowned in the lake last night."

Nora stared at her for a minute, and Bree waited for shock or worry to cross her face. But instead, she burst out laughing.

"Quin almost drowning! That's the most ridiculous thing I've ever heard!"

"B-but . . . I found him on the beach," Bree stammered, and she told Nora the whole story of what had happened.

But even after she'd heard it all, Nora just shook

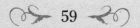

her head. "I don't know what happened to Quin, but if he says he almost drowned, he's telling a big fat lie. He's the strongest swimmer in the whole town. His last name *means* 'Stream Horse,' as in a horse made for swimming. His family was born for the water." She swirled her toes in the lake. "Besides, nobody's drowned in this lake for fifty years. But you won't hear anybody in town talk about that story. It still freaks people out."

"Why?" Bree's heart quickened. "What happened?"

"Nobody ever knew for sure," Nora said. "One summer, six kids drowned in one month. It was the strangest thing." She stared out at the lake. "Doctors said they were sleepwalking or something. Whatever it was, these kids just left their beds in the middle of the night and wandered out to the lake. The next morning they were gone. Each time it happened, they dragged the lake, and sure enough, found each one of their bodies. It was only Thomas Stromhest they never found."

"Thomas Stromhest?" Bree said quietly, recognizing the name from something her aunt had said to her before. "Was he related to Quin?"

Nora nodded. "Quin never met him, but Thomas was Arvid's brother, so that would've made him

Quin's great-uncle. The last time anyone saw him was on Midsummer's Eve, fifty years ago. They never knew for sure what happened to him. I guess everyone figured that he drowned just like the other kids."

"That's pretty creepy," Bree said, feeling a sudden chill, even though the sun was still shining brightly.

"Yeah," Nora said, kicking a wave and sending up a small splash of water. "Anyway, people around here are superstitious, and for a while there were stories about some sort of lake creature killing the kids. Nobody believes ridiculous stuff like that anymore, except for maybe your aunt. I heard she thinks the drownings all had to do with some ancient curse. But it's funny. Even though nobody else believes that, they don't ever talk about what happened either. It's like they think it'll bring bad luck or something." She grinned, then added in a spooky voice, "Maybe we should stop talking about it before the lake monster attacks again!"

"Yeah." Bree laughed, but a clamminess had crept over her while Nora was talking, and it was tough to shake. As fascinating as Nora's tale had been, Bree really *did* need a subject change. "So . . . what's Midsummer's Eve?"

Nora gawked at her. "Only the coolest part of being Norwegian-American. Midsummer's Eve is the summer solstice. It's not this coming Saturday but the one after that. The whole town comes down to a spot on the lake for a big party. There's a fish bake, music, games, swimming, and dancing around a maypole. We have a huge bonfire, and there are fireworks over the lake afterward."

"Sounds like fun," Bree said. "Except for maybe the fish bake part. Ick."

"Well, you probably won't think it's as fun as your concerts in Central Park, but it's the coolest thing this town does. You'll see." Nora smiled, then pointed to the water. "So, are we *ever* going to go swimming or what?"

"Definitely," Bree said.

She started to wade in, trying not to make a face at the slimy lake bottom, but Nora ran into the water suddenly, laughing.

"Come on!" she hollered. "Last one in has to row home!"

Bree ran after her, laughing and shouting, "You better let me win or we won't be back to town until winter!"

Bree clicked off her bedside lamp and slid under the covers, smiling. She was stiff and tired, but it was a good kind of tired, the kind that came from being out in the sunshine and water all day. After sitting through Aunt Hedda's tight-lipped silence at dinner, Bree missed Nora's chatty perkiness. She'd had a great time with Nora, and when they'd gotten back to Aunt Hedda's, they'd had even more fun trying Bree's clothes on Nora and working on her "fashion deficiency," as Nora called it. Quin had been long gone by then, and when Bree had asked Aunt Hedda about him, she just mumbled something about him needing to get back to Arvid. Her aunt hadn't mentioned Quin again for the rest of the night either.

Now, lying awake in the darkness, Bree's mind swirled with questions about the town and its people. Between the dragonheads, Quin's strange behavior, the mysterious midnight music, and stories about drownings and lake monsters, Bree didn't know whether she was visiting another state or another planet.

She was busy puzzling over these things when she heard the screen door on the porch creak open and closed. She swung her legs out of bed and peered out the window. Aunt Hedda was making her way down the outside stairs with a flashlight in one hand and one of her houseguests, a huge rat, in the other. The rat was writhing and squealing wildly.

Aunt Hedda walked toward the lake, soon disappearing into the tall grass. Bree waited for her to come back, but minutes passed, and there was no sign of her. Finally, about fifteen minutes later, her aunt crested the hill again. This time, she had the flashlight, but the rat was gone.

Bree flopped back into bed, her mind racing. What could her aunt possibly have been doing with the rat in the middle of the night? Had she set it free down by the lake? That seemed to be the most logical explanation, but a nagging voice inside her told Bree there was more to it than that. She'd *done* something with the rat. But . . . what?

A sick feeling settled in the pit of Bree's stomach, and she closed her eyes, wanting sleep to come so she could stop thinking the awful thoughts that were surfacing. But when sleep finally arrived, the music came with it, whispering through her dreams, lulling her, luring her. She had to fight with everything inside her to keep from following it outside again. But this time, she managed to stop herself. Because with all she'd heard about and seen today, she was starting to think that maybe her aunt was right, after all. Maybe Midnight Lake *was* dangerous after dark.

CHAPTER SIX

The fog was so thick it practically rippled around her as she walked, like water. This was only her third day here, but already Bree noticed how changeable the lake was — one minute crystal clear and glimmering with sunlight, the next steeped in shadows and mist. She brushed away the water droplets clinging to her hair and waded through the whiteness toward the pebbly beach. Thanks to her outing yesterday with Nora, she was starting to see Midnight Lake in a whole different light. It was rugged, sure, but it was beautiful, too, and filled with cool plants and animals to draw. In fact, she'd even woken up before dawn this morning craving her charcoal pencils and sketchbook, and she'd headed for the lake, hoping that if she waited long enough beside the water, some sort of subject — human or animal — would come along for her to draw. Of course, that didn't mean she'd forgiven her parents for shipping her off to Aunt Hedda for the summer. She was eccentric and sour, and that was putting it mildly. But still, even if Bree didn't mesh with her aunt, maybe it wouldn't be so bad to be here, after all.

She crested the last dune, smiling and humming the melody that had woven its way through her dreams. But the second the beach came into view, the notes died on her lips. A pile of bones was visible from where she stood, ghostly white splinters against the gray backdrop of the lapping waves.

Bitter bile rose in her throat as understanding dawned on her, but she still moved in for a closer look, wanting to know with certainty that what she suspected was true. She wasn't a scientist, she knew, but this skeleton looked alarmingly close to the right size and shape for a large . . . rat.

Bree sank onto the rocks, her breath coming quick and panicky. So this had been the rat's fate. Aunt Hedda had brought the rat down to the water to — ugh, she could barely think it — dispose of it. But if that was true, then how had her aunt done it? Why wasn't there any fur, or any (ick!) skin, left on the poor animal?

Bree was fighting not to gag when Aunt Hedda's voice came sharply from the house.

"Bree! Breakfast!"

Bree shuddered, then turned away from the dead rat and made her way to the house, wondering how she'd ever be able to stomach whatever gelatinous Norwegian dish her aunt was serving up today. But to her immense relief, when she sat down at the kitchen table, there was a golden-brown waffle on her plate, drenched in syrup.

"You don't seem to like the herring much," her aunt said, attempting a stiff smile. "I thought waffles might be more up your alley."

"Thanks," Bree said appreciatively. Even though her stomach was still churning from the rat, she forced herself to eat most of the waffle, anyway. If her aunt thought she didn't like it, who knew what else she'd try for breakfast tomorrow?

"So," Aunt Hedda said stiltedly, "I thought maybe if you weren't busy this morning, I could show you some of the old family albums. I have some photos of your great-great-grandparents I thought you might like to see. They were the first generation of Danielsens to live at Midnight Lake."

Bree swallowed thickly, her heart quickening. She should've been happy. After all, it was the first real attempt at bonding her great-aunt had made with her since she'd arrived. But instead, all she felt was a leaden dread at the prospect of spending the entire morning with a woman who had just done — well, whatever she'd done — to that rat. Not that Bree especially loved rats. Actually, as a general rule, they grossed her out. No, what bothered her more was that there was something abnormal — disturbing, even — about her aunt's behavior. Keeping wild animals in cages on your front porch was not something the average sane person would do. But . . . killing them? Well, that was even crazier. So Bree did what she thought she had to do. She lied.

"That sounds great," Bree said, trying to make her voice sound as enthusiastic as possible. "But actually, I was going to walk over to Anna's coffee shop. I need to check out some books for my summer reading list, and I wanted to e-mail Fiona and some of my other friends back home." She paused, unable to meet her aunt's gaze. "If that's okay."

Aunt Hedda cleared her throat loudly and instantly stood up to collect the breakfast dishes. "Of course," she mumbled. "As long as you're staying busy, that's all that matters. You have to keep up with all that schoolwork. Your father's told me all the nonsense about school admissions. And I suppose family histories just don't mean as much to younger generations these days." Her mouth was set in a tight line, and Bree thought she detected the slightest hint of disappointment in her aunt's voice.

"I'd love to hear about the family some other time, though," Bree said, a stab of guilt striking her heart. "Anytime."

Her aunt waved her away from the breakfast table. "Go on, then. The photo albums aren't going anywhere."

"Okay," Bree said, grabbing her bag and sketch-book. "I'll be back later."

But as Bree bounced down the stairs alongside the house, her relief was spoiled by shame, and she paused on the bottom step. She could go back inside and make an effort with her aunt. But . . . no. She had the entire rest of the summer to visit with her aunt. Right now, all she wanted to do was forget what she'd seen on the beach. Forget the houseguests, the bones, the blood moon. Forget her aunt's bizarre behavior. For a few hours, she wanted to remember what it felt like to just be Bree, the fun, sun-seeking New Yorker who'd never wanted to come here in the first place.

Bree heard the music long before she saw where it was coming from. The tune was lively and fun, tripping along in the air, tickling her ears and tempting her toes to tap the beat. It was the kind of music you just had to dance to, and within seconds of hearing it, Bree was stepping in time to it, bouncing down the trail beside the lake with a grin on her face, feeling happier than she had all morning. The music reeled faster, and Bree picked up the pace to keep up with it, her heart thrilled to hear it growing louder with each step she took.

Then Bree rounded the bend to Arvid Stromhest's house and her heart clattered to a stop. Quin sat on the rocks below the house, his eyes half closed, a slow smile lifting the corners of his mouth. The fiddle tucked under his chin looked more like an extension of him than any kind of separate instrument, and his bow raced across those strings in a frenzied blur. Quin wasn't just playing music; he was bringing it to life.

Bree froze where she stood, afraid if she moved one muscle, Quin would see her, and the spell would be broken. And sure enough, a twig under her shoe snapped, Quin's eyes flew open, stormy with surprise, and the bow let out a screech of protest.

"I'm sorry," Bree said instantly, blushing. She probably looked like a horrible snoop right now, and that wasn't going to help much to get her back on his good side. "I didn't mean to catch you off guard."

She held her breath, not sure what to expect from Quin after he'd been so snappish with her yesterday.

But he just gave her a teasing smile and said, "Eavesdropping, huh?" He looked tired and pale, but his eyes had regained some of their playful glint, even if there were slight shadows underneath them now.

"I was just on my way to town and I heard the music." She smiled. "You're amazing. How did you learn to play like that?"

Quin shrugged. "My grandpa plays, and I mostly just picked it up by watching him, I guess. But he swears I was fiddling before I could walk or talk, with no help from him. He says we come from a long line of natural-born musicians."

"Could you play something else?" Bree asked, sitting down on the rocks next to him. "Please?" She was surprised by how pleading her voice sounded, and how much she really wished he would start playing again.

Quin ran his hand over his fiddle, seeming to consider, but then he shook his head. "Sorry. I have to restring it first." He held it out to her, showing her two snapped strings. "Sometimes that happens when I get a little carried away."

"Too bad," Bree said, feeling a sudden, sharp disappointment. "I'd love to hear more."

Quin shrugged. "I'm sure you can hear way better anytime you want at the concert halls in New York, right?" He said it with a slight edge in his voice, as if he was waiting to see if she'd start bragging about all the great music and culture Manhattan had to offer. Bree bristled slightly. She didn't know why he'd assume she'd make comparisons like that.

"I've never heard anything like your music before," Bree said with complete honesty.

"Hmmm, in that case, I might have to start charging admission." His eyes met hers, and they both giggled.

"I'm glad you're feeling better," Bree said quietly. "After yesterday, I mean."

Quin nodded, studying the rocks at his feet intensely. "I know I was sort of obnoxious to you. I'm sorry. I felt pretty lousy after everything."

"So what happened, anyway?" Bree asked.

"I don't know," he said. "I guess I panicked when I fell out of the boat and swallowed some water. That's all."

"That's weird," Bree said, watching his face closely, "because Nora told me you're the best swimmer in town."

The second the words left Bree's mouth, Quin's face walled up.

"Look, maybe I don't remember what happened, okay?" He said it too quickly and too loudly, as if he actually remembered *everything* that had happened. He just didn't *want* to remember.

He picked up a rock and launched it toward the lake, scowling at the water. "The whole thing was just . . . stupid." He blew a strand of wiry hair from his forehead. "I'm sick of talking about it."

"Sorry," Bree said quietly, her cheeks warming. "I shouldn't have said anything." Frustration tightened her stomach. How did she always manage to say the wrong things around him? She stood up. "I should probably get going, anyway. I'm heading into town, and I promised Aunt Hedda I'd be back at the house for lunch." She started to pick her way down the rocks. "I'll see you later."

She'd just reached the trail again when Quin called out to her.

"Wait!" he said, scrambling down the rocks toward her. His scowl was gone, replaced with an apologetic smile. "I didn't mean to sound like that. . . . I just can't . . ." He shook his head at the ground, as if he were having an argument with himself. Then he sighed and said, "Can I come along with you?"

"S-sure," Bree stammered, feeling a wave of happiness through her confusion. One minute he was snapping at her and the next inviting himself to hang out with her. She knew all boys acted weird around girls sometimes, but this was ridiculous. She waited for him as he put away his fiddle, and then they walked the rest of the way to town.

Bree soon discovered that once she quit pressing him about his accident, talking to Quin was easy. He asked her about her sketchbook, and even seemed impressed when she showed him a few of her drawings. He told her about his grandpa and how he'd raised Quin from a baby, and she told him about her parents and her friends back in the city. A glimmer of the teasing Quin with the laughing eyes came back, and Bree was enjoying talking to him so much that she was disappointed when they reached Anna's Bookstop Coffee Shop. Because the second Nora rushed out to greet them, the openness on Quin's face shut up tight.

"Well?" Nora said, striking a pose on the sidewalk in Capri jeggings and a belted, beaded tunic top. "What do you think of the outfit?"

"It's fabulous," Bree said. "My clothes look great on you, if I do say so myself."

"Thank you!" Nora giggled. "I feel like a whole new metropolitan me."

"I thought the old you was just fine," Quin mumbled.

"Of course you did. Because boys have no fashion sense at all," Nora said dramatically. "No offense," she added, for Quin's benefit. Then she pulled them into the store. "I'm so glad you guys are here!"

"I am, too!" Bree said. "I *so* need a dose of civilization." She was just being truthful, but as soon as she said it, she felt Quin stiffen beside her. "Fiona probably thinks I'm on some missing-persons list by now. I haven't e-mailed her at all yet!"

"You'll just have to explain to her that computers haven't been introduced to us backwoods people yet," Quin said drily, giving Bree a sharp look. "Since we're so uncivilized, you know."

Bree stared at him. Where had *that* come from? "I didn't mean it like that. I —"

"Oh, forget about it," Nora said, acting as if she hadn't heard Quin's sarcastic comment, or if she had, she didn't care. "E-mail can wait. Mom's on the verge of a nervous breakdown. She volunteered to do the decorations for the Midsummer's Eve Festival, and she — well, *me* — need helpers."

Anna nodded from the sales counter, where she and Kari were perched on stools eating Danishes. "I don't know what got into me," Anna said, "But now I have to make garlands for a maypole and paint a bunch of wooden backdrops for silly photos. And I have to do it all while I run the shop."

"Well, I'll check with Aunt Hedda, but I'm sure I can help out," Bree said quickly with a smile. After all, Aunt Hedda had said she wanted Bree to stay busy, and this would be the perfect excuse to get out of that.

"I can help, too," Quin said, a little more reluctantly. "As long as we work during the day. I have to help Grandpa with the chores."

Anna clapped her hands. "Great!" She grinned. "Oh, that's such a relief. And I know you will do a terrific job. I was thinking we could all have a picnic Saturday afternoon at the cove to start planning things out. Hedda and Arvid should come, too. They're our oldest town residents, and they'll be able to give us some wonderful ideas, I'm sure."

"We can't come," Quin said flatly. "Grandpa doesn't go out on the water anymore, and he won't want me out by myself after dark."

"Oh, that's too bad," Anna said. But then she turned to Bree. "I hope Hedda will join us. Did you know she's an expert on our Midsummer's Eve traditions? A few years ago some party poopers wanted to get rid of the bonfire. They didn't think it was safe. But Hedda wouldn't hear of losing the bonfire. She put up quite a fight."

Bree giggled at the vision of her tough aunt waging war against the town's fire-safety department. Leave it to her aunt to stir up trouble. "Why did she care so much about it?"

Anna smiled. "Oh, it's an old Norwegian superstition that Midsummer's Eve is a time when wicked spirits and creatures come out of their hiding places to cause trouble. Bonfires are built to keep them away."

"Wow," Bree said, rolling her eyes. "That's so dark ages."

"No, it's not!" Kari piped up around a mouthful of Danish. "It's real! Quin's grandpa knows about the creatures. Mr. Stromhest's brother, Thomas, got killed by one. Isn't that right, Quin?"

Bree looked at Quin, and saw him turn three shades paler, his mouth set in a bitter line.

"Kari, hush!" Anna whispered, but it was too late. Quin was already hurrying out of the shop.

"I have to go," he said, blowing through the door without looking back at the stunned faces he was leaving behind him.

"Quin!" Bree called, hurrying after him as Anna scolded Kari. "Wait up!" She caught up with him a half a block later. She touched him lightly on the shoulder, and he whirled around to face her.

"Don't you have some e-mails to write?" he said with a challenging glare.

"What's going on?" she asked, ignoring the dig. "You know Kari doesn't have a clue what she's talking about. She's only five."

"It's not Kari. Kari's smarter than a lot of people in this town. It's you. You think this town is a complete joke." He ran a hand through his hair, making it even more tousled. "You act like it's such a tragedy not to have your cell phone and e-mails, and then laugh about us being stuck in the dark ages."

Bree gave a short laugh. "Come on. Don't you think it's sort of ridiculous that the town isn't more . . . techno-savvy? And that people here talk about storybook monsters like they're real? You have to admit it's a little old-fashioned."

He stared at her, his slate eyes roiling with anger. "So what if it is? Maybe we need our bonfires. Maybe things happen here that don't happen in New York. Things you don't want to write home about."

"What are you talking about?" Bree threw up her hands. "Does anyone ever say anything that makes sense around here?" First it was her aunt spouting gibberish about blood moons and evil spirits, and now Quin with bonfires? Yeesh.

He kicked at the sidewalk and then trudged away down the street. "Never mind," he muttered angrily as he left. "Forget I said anything about it."

But Bree couldn't forget about it. After making up excuses for Quin's odd behavior to Nora and her mom, and sending quick e-mails to her parents and Fiona, Bree walked back home alone, replaying her conversations with Quin over and over again in her head, trying to figure out what she'd done wrong.

But then, when a pitch-black, moonless night descended, she began to think she had even bigger problems. Because again her aunt made her nocturnal trip to the lake, and this time Bree followed. She watched Aunt Hedda tie the badger's leash to a stake in the ground near the water's edge. She watched Aunt Hedda leave the badger growling and struggling to free itself. Bree made sure to beat her aunt back to the house so she wouldn't suspect she'd ever been out. But at first light, Bree went back to the beach to find the tattered leash ripped and empty.

It took half of Thursday morning and a hike around the lake to find it, but she finally did. A pile of bones washed up a mile down shore. And then she knew beyond a doubt. She knew what Quin had been trying, but unable, to say. There was something twisted happening in Midnight Lake. Because Aunt Hedda wasn't killing the houseguests herself. She was leaving them for someone — or *something* — else to devour.

CHAPTER SEVEN

The knock on Bree's door came Friday morning while her bedroom was still steeped in shadows, and she thought for a minute that she must have dreamed it. But then it came again, and Aunt Hedda's face poked around the door.

"Time to get dressed," her aunt said. "There's a surprise for you in the kitchen. Hurry up now, while the fish are still biting."

A surprise? She wasn't sure she wanted any more of her aunt's surprises, especially if they involved more dead animals. And what was that she'd said about fish? Bree sat up and looked at the clock. Five A.M. Groan. What kind of new torture was this? She rubbed her eyes, trying to shake off the heaviness of sleep. She'd tossed and turned for hours last night, either having nightmares about bleached bones or fighting the urge to follow the music. She'd heard it every night since the blood moon, and each time she found it harder and harder to ignore.

She dressed as quickly as she could with her limbs of lead, and then, with eyes half closed, made her way to the kitchen.

"Surprise!" Aunt Hedda said, a Strawberry Shortcake fishing pole in her hand and a proud smile on her face that was so unlike her it was all Bree could do to keep from gawking.

"Do you like it?" Her aunt held the pole out to her. "I picked it up for you yesterday at the bait-and-tackle shop. Your dad was quite the fisherman as a boy. And when Quin called yesterday to see if you could go fishing with him today, I knew you couldn't go without a proper pole."

"It's . . ." *Totally babyish*, she thought, but she could never say that. After all, it was a first to have her aunt acting so . . . friendly. She didn't want to ruin this weird but touching moment. "It's . . . great. Thanks." She took the pole tentatively, trying not to think about how many five-year-olds owned the very same one. Well, at least she was three thousand miles away from any friends who could laugh at it. Oh no . . . except . . .

"Quin?" Bree said in disbelief, finally processing the other part of what Aunt Hedda had said. "*Quin* wants to take me fishing?" How was that even possible when two days ago, Quin had stormed off in a rage?

Aunt Hedda nodded. "It was all his idea, and it's a great one. He could use a real friend right now. And as for you, you can't spend all your time just sketching the great outdoors. You need to live a little in them, too. I've packed a cooler with sandwiches for you to take along."

Bree was about to give Aunt Hedda a million and one reasons why fishing with Quin was a *very* bad idea. Like for starters, the fact that he hadn't spoken a word to her since his blowup on Wednesday and was probably more likely to throw her overboard than help her learn to fish. But before Bree could say another word, Quin himself was knocking on the back door, peering through the screen with a playful grin.

"I hope you're ready to catch a monster," he said lightly, as if nothing about this was even remotely unusual.

"Oh, she is," her aunt said, and after plunking the cooler into her arms, gave Bree a gentle nudge out the door.

*   *   *

Bree waited until they were safely out of earshot of the house and nearing the dock in front of Quin's house, and then let it all out.

"What is going on?" She spun on Quin, glaring at him. "I don't get you. You blew up at me out of nowhere the other day, and now you're pretending it didn't even happen."

"I know it happened," Quin said quietly, his smile dimming. "I'm sorry I lost it with you. I shouldn't have." He sighed. "I've had some kind of serious stuff happening lately, but it's not your problem." He shrugged. "I thought I could take you fishing to make it up to you."

Bree snorted a laugh. "Because I *love* fishing so much?"

"You've never *been* fishing. See, that's part of why I got mad before." Quin raised an eyebrow at her. "I just get sick of all the narrow-mindedness sometimes."

Bree gaped at him. "Wait . . . you think *I'm* narrow-minded?"

"About Midnight Lake?" Quin nodded. "Yeah. You think this town is pathetic and boring."

"I never said that —" Bree said.

"Maybe not in those exact words," Quin said, walking down the dock toward a pretty, honey-colored boat with a small motor on its back. "But all that talk about you dying for some civilization? And laughing at how outdated we are? Did you ever think about how that makes you sound to people around here? Like some stuck-up city girl who can't survive five minutes without her cell phone."

"But that's not who I am," Bree said. She'd never thought about it that way before. But to the locals, maybe she *did* seem that way. "This town is like some warped club you need a secret password to become a part of. I bet nobody here thinks I'm even worthy of being here. You talk about me jumping to conclusions. What about what you all think about *me*?"

"So, prove me wrong," Quin said, jumping into the boat and pointing to the other seat. "I want to see you fish with that preschool pole of yours . . . right now."

Bree didn't even hesitate. She was *not* going to let him get away with thinking she was a cosmopolitan prima donna. No way. Especially when *he* was the one with the attitude problem. She clambered onto the boat, and locked eyes with him and smiled. "What are you waiting for? Let's go."

"I've got another one!" Quin said again, for at least the tenth time. "Quick, get the net!"

Bree handed him the net, rolling her eyes. "I thought *I* was supposed to be fishing, too. All I'm doing is netting *your* fish."

Quin grinned as he plopped another fish into his cooler. "You should've gotten at least one by now."

"Yeah, well, all the fish are on *your* side of the boat," she said, recasting her line yet again. "Are you sure you can't cheat at fishing? Because fish are flocking to you and avoiding me like the plague."

"Maybe the fish have just outgrown Strawberry Shortcake," Quin teased, and then laughed when Bree slugged him on the arm.

"Watch it or I'll throw you overboard," Bree growled.

"I'd like to see you try it," Quin taunted. He laughed, and his silver eyes glittered crystalline in the sunlight. Bree had a hard time tearing her own away, and when she finally did, she was blushing.

But she was laughing, too. She hadn't caught a

single fish yet (and she still wasn't entirely sure she wanted to), but she was having a great time. They'd been out on the water for a couple of hours, and in that time she'd seen what an amazing fisherman Quin was. He knew all the best fishing spots — a few times she could've sworn she saw whole schools of fish following the boat as if they actually *wanted* Quin to catch them.

"So, what's your secret?" Bree said jokingly as Quin cast his line out again into the sparkling water.

But instead of giving a funny comeback, like she'd expected, Quin suddenly blanched, his moonlight eyes changing to thunderclouds. "You don't want to know," he whispered harshly. The response was so instant and misplaced that Bree felt the nigglings of an inexplicable fear.

"No," she said, forcing a light laugh. "I meant the secret to your *fishing*."

Quin blinked blankly, and then his face relaxed. "Oh." He laughed halfheartedly. "Yeah. I knew that." He stared out at the water for a minute, then looked back at Bree. "Maybe it's just that I know the water, and it knows me. Sort of like I belong to it, if that makes sense."

"I get that," Bree said with a nod. "That's how I feel about New York." Suddenly, she felt a series of tiny pops on her fishing line, and then a firm tug. "Hey," she said as her bobber ducked under the water's surface. Her heart surged with excitement. "Hey! I think I have one!"

She jumped up out of her seat, and as soon as she did, she realized her mistake. The boat tipped violently to one side, and she staggered backward, losing her footing. She would've gone over the side if Quin hadn't grabbed her at the last second and pulled her back. She landed in the bottom of the boat, mostly on top of Quin, who'd broken her fall. It was only after she'd caught her breath that she realized that her head was buried in his shoulder, his arms wrapped firmly around her waist.

"You mean you *had* one," Quin said with a smile, his face so near hers she could feel the warmth of his breath on her cheek. A heady jolt of electricity raced through her, but then Quin shifted away, helping her back onto her seat.

"Sorry," she said, hoping her face didn't look as fiery as it felt.

"No problem," Quin said. He held up her pole,

showing her the snapped fishing line. "Except that I don't have any spare hooks." He checked his watch. "We should probably be heading back, anyway. I have to help Grandpa with dinner tonight." He started the motor and turned the boat toward the shore. Then he nodded at the fish still left in the water. "You just made their day."

Bree giggled. "Oh, well. I'd rather not see my food swimming around before eating it, anyway."

They rode the rest of the way back to shore in amicable silence, and when Bree climbed out of the boat, she actually felt disappointed that their fishing trip was ending. And it had nothing to do with the fact that she hadn't caught any fish.

"Thanks for taking me along today," she said as Quin tied up the boat. "It was really fun."

Quin nodded. "It was, although it might've been more fun if you'd actually gone *into* the water."

"Very funny," Bree said. "Well, if you come along on the picnic tomorrow, you'll see it happen for real."

Quin shook his head. "I wish I could. But you won't be back until after dark. And, well, ever since I had that accident, Grandpa doesn't like me being out on the water at night." He smiled. "But don't worry.

It's a small town. You'll see me around, probably a lot sooner than you want to."

Bree laughed, and started to walk up the dock, but then she hesitated. There was something she needed to know. "Hey," she said quietly, "do you really think I'm a stuck-up city girl?"

"Nah," he said. "I just wanted to see if I could sucker you into gutting my fish for me."

"Not a chance." Bree laughed.

Quin's smile shifted into seriousness. "Actually, I think you belong here. More than you'd ever believe you do." He brought his eyes up to meet hers, looking at her with such confidence that she felt as if he'd learned some secret truth about her that even *she* didn't know. And as she walked back home, she wondered if the truth had anything to do with the thrill she'd felt when his arms had caught her, pulling her back from the water's edge.

CHAPTER EIGHT

Bree lay back on her beach towel, listening to Nora read an article about the latest lip-gloss trends in *Teen People*, relishing the sun's warmth on her face. The weather had turned out to be absolutely perfect for their picnic, warmer and sunnier than any day Bree'd had on the lake so far. The water in the cove felt wonderful, too, and she, Nora, and Kari had been swimming almost nonstop since they'd arrived. Even Aunt Hedda, much to Bree's amazement, had slipped off her boots and waded up to her ankles in the water.

And when she'd caught Bree and Nora staring at her, she'd snapped, "Yes, I do possess feet, albeit ugly ones."

Everyone had burst out laughing, and even Aunt Hedda had cracked a dry smile. The picnic seemed to be putting everyone in a great mood. Bree and Nora had come up with some great ideas for the Midsummer's Eve decorations, and they were planning to get together on Monday to paint the photo stands. The only thing that could have possibly made the afternoon any better was if Quin had come along. Bree had caught herself daydreaming about their fishing trip together a few times, but each time she'd shaken herself out of it by reminding herself of his unpredictable mood swings. True, the fact that he called her on some of her behavior was infuriating, but she also liked his honesty and his wicked sense of humor. And today, it seemed that every time she looked out at the lake, Quin's face popped into her mind.

"Okay, who's ready to eat?" Anna called from where she was sitting on a huge picnic blanket with Aunt Hedda, spreading out paper plates and food.

"We are!" Nora belted out, pulling Bree up off her towel. "Studying up on fashion trends is hard work. I've worked up an appetite."

"I'm starving, too," Bree said as they sat down on the blanket. Kari came tumbling out of the lake and plopped down in between Nora and Bree, sprinkling both of them with water.

"Here's your sandwich, Bree." Aunt Hedda handed her tough-looking bread slices with some pungent-smelling unidentifiable meat in the middle.

"Thanks," Bree said tentatively, eyeing the sandwich suspiciously. Whatever was inside didn't look *or* smell good. "Um . . . what is it?"

"Mutton sausage," her aunt said. "A Norwegian specialty. Give it a try."

Bree glanced at Nora and Kari, both of whom were wolfing down the peanut butter and jelly sandwiches Anna had made for them. Bree swallowed, remembering Quin's words yesterday. She didn't want to be a food snob, especially when she'd never even given her aunt's sandwich a try. So she braced herself, lifted the sandwich to her mouth, and took a big bite. It was salty, with spices that tasted foreign to her, but all in all, it wasn't too bad.

"Good girl," her aunt said, nodding in appreciation. "Now, would you like your *real* sandwich?"

Bree blinked in confusion. "But . . . I thought this was mine."

"No, it's mine," Aunt Hedda said. Nora burst into giggles as Aunt Hedda scooped the sausage sandwich up and handed Bree a PB&J. "I just wanted to see if you'd give it a try. And you did, with true Norwegian grit. I knew it was buried in you somewhere."

Bree smiled. "I . . . I guess so."

"Well, then," Aunt Hedda said. "You don't have to eat the mutton, unless of course, you want to."

"No!" Bree said quickly, and then before she could catch herself, she blurted out, "It was completely disgusting."

She cringed inwardly, wondering if Aunt Hedda would scold her for being rude. But instead, her aunt threw back her head and gave a big belly laugh. "There's that grit again. I love it."

Bree laughed, feeling an unexpected rush of pride at her aunt's approval. She hadn't thought she'd cared that much what her aunt thought about her until that moment. But maybe she'd been wrong.

She scarfed down her sandwich and then had two helpings of her aunt's cloudberry cream, a delicious dessert made of special mountain berries from the "old country," as her aunt called it. Bree was scraping the last spoonful out of her cup when Kari jumped up and ran full tilt into the water and Nora jumped up to follow her.

"Come on, Bree," Nora said. "Let's get back in."

Bree leaped to her feet, but Aunt Hedda put out her hand to stop them.

"Only a few more minutes in the water," she said, her eyes on the setting sun. "It's getting late and it'll be dusk soon."

"It's fine, Hedda," Anna said. "There's still plenty of light. Let them have some fun."

Her aunt's mouth fused into a firm line, but she didn't say anything else as Bree raced after Nora and Kari into the water. She splashed through the lapping waves and dove in, the refreshingly cold water rippling over her. She laughed and swam under Nora's feet, grabbing her toes to make her yelp. Then she and Nora both started a splashing war with Kari. She lost all track of time until her aunt's firm voice cut through her fun.

"Bree!" Aunt Hedda's voice was edged with a sharpness. "It's getting dark, and I have to get home to do some chores. It's time to get out of the water now!"

Bree looked up to see the purple dusk deepening, the first stars winking into the sky.

"Just a few more minutes!" Bree called. "Please."

"Come on!" Nora seconded. "It's not even that dark yet."

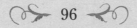

"Oh, let them play until I finish packing up," Anna said as she started loading up the boat with their picnic supplies.

"No," her aunt said with a severity that made Anna (and everyone else) look at her in surprise. "I really must get home. And, well, it's just not safe for them to stay in the water after dark."

"What's up with Aunt Worrywart?" Nora whispered to Bree. "Does she think we need floaties or something?"

"I don't know," Bree said, but she guessed that by "chores" her aunt meant taking another houseguest out to be eaten. Not that she'd ever mention that to another living soul, unless she wanted her aunt labeled the town crazy.

"Stop this foolishness," her aunt suddenly barked. "There are things that come out at night that should never have to be reckoned with."

Bree's face burned. What was her aunt *doing*? She'd been acting so . . . normal earlier. And now this. Bree just wanted to make her stop before it got any more embarrassing. "It's all right," Bree said, starting toward shore. "I'm coming."

Nora and Kari, on the other hand, stayed in the water, splashing and playing. "I'm never coming out,"

Kari sing-songed, sticking out her tongue at Aunt Hedda and Anna. "Not in a million years."

"Come on, girls," Anna said, holding out towels. "Listen, now."

"No!" Kari shouted, but then seconds later, her laughter curdled into a scream. Bree gasped as Nora came running out of the dark water with Kari, who was clutching her calf.

"Something bit me!" Kari wailed. "It stings so bad!"

"What on earth could've bitten you?" Anna said, but then she gently lifted Kari's hand from her calf to reveal a dozen bleeding teeth marks.

"Those look weird," Nora whispered. "They look . . . human."

Bree leaned closer and saw that Nora was right. Except for two fanglike puncture wounds, the marks looked like a person had made them. Seriously creepy.

"I have just the thing for that sort of bite," Aunt Hedda said calmly, "but we need to get back to the house right away, before her pain gets worse."

Nobody ignored her this time, and after scrambling for the last of their supplies, they were on the boat racing across the lake. Once they were back at the house, Aunt Hedda put a bitter-smelling herbal cream on Kari's leg and wrapped it in a bandage, and soon Kari's tears had dried and she was back to pestering Nora again. Bree was impressed by her aunt's quick remedy, but her bedside manner was horrible. The whole time she was washing and dressing Kari's wound, she was distracted, glancing toward the porch and her houseguests. And Anna had to ask Hedda several times about how often to apply more cream before she actually heard and answered. The good-byes were awkward, with no one sure exactly what had happened, and no one wanting to meet one another's eyes.

As soon as Anna's taillights disappeared down the drive, Aunt Hedda turned away from the door and grumbled, "It's late. I'm going to bed."

"Okay," Bree said quietly. "Good night."

But Aunt Hedda acted as if she hadn't even heard her. "I tried to warn them," she mumbled under her breath, shaking her head. "And now I missed the feeding. Stupid. *Stupid*."

Bree stared at her aunt as she walked down the hallway to her bedroom still mumbling to herself, and a sickly sweat pricked her neck. A thought she'd been trying to ignore pushed its way to the surface.

Maybe her aunt wasn't a grumpy old woman; maybe she was a crazy one.

The crackling and crunching of gravel woke her early Sunday morning, and Bree glanced blearily out her window to see a large, official-looking truck pulling into the driveway. Aunt Hedda seemed to have been waiting for it, because she was already outside, waving the uniformed man toward the lake as soon as he stepped out of the truck's cab. The man slipped on a pair of heavy work gloves, grabbed an industrial garbage bag out of the truck, and walked away with her aunt. *What now?* Bree thought, scrambling to get dressed so she could follow them.

In record time, she made it out of the house and down to the dirt trail. Soon she spotted Aunt Hedda and the man in quiet, deep conversation, studying something in front of them on the ground.

"I thought it best to call Parks and Wildlife right away," Aunt Hedda was saying. "It's just not sanitary to leave it on the beach."

"Of course not. I'm happy to help. Comes with the territory." The man motioned to his badge, and Bree guessed he must be some sort of game warden.

He shook his head. "It's just incredible to me that no one noticed the body before now. It's probably been out here for weeks. Just look at it . . . there's nothing left but bones."

Instantly, clamminess crawled over Bree's skin. After the awful things she'd already found washed up on the beach, she wasn't sure she wanted to see this. But she forced herself to step closer, until she could clearly see the huge skeleton of a deer at the water's edge.

The sharp gasp came before she could stop it, and her aunt spun around the second she heard it.

"Bree, go back to the house," she said flatly. "This doesn't concern you."

"But . . . what happened?" Bree asked. "How did it get here?"

"Oh, most likely a wolf pack, or maybe a bear," the game warden said. He smiled kindly at her. "But don't you worry about that now. They don't ever bother people." He held up the garbage bag he was holding. "Well, I'll get started taking care of this, and you ladies will have your lovely beach back in no time."

"Thank you, Officer Trent," Aunt Hedda said. "I'll have a cup of coffee ready for you when you've finished." She slipped her arm around Bree and turned her away, keeping a firm grip on her shoulder until they were back at the house. But although Bree allowed herself to be led without causing a scene, she wasn't about to let what she'd seen go.

"Do you think wolves really did that?" she asked as her aunt spooned grounds into the filter of the coffeemaker.

"Of course," snapped her aunt. "Why ask such a silly question?"

"I don't know," Bree said. "It's just . . . those aren't the only bones I've seen along the lake, and I was wondering . . ."

Her aunt jerked her head toward Bree, her sharp gaze burning into her. "What bones? Why didn't you tell me that before?"

Bree shrugged. "I don't know," she said, flustered. "I didn't think it mattered before. I'm sorry." Bree dropped her eyes to the floor, not understanding where the sudden harshness in her aunt's tone was coming from.

"It's all right," Hedda said, turning back to the coffeepot. But Bree noticed that there was a slight quiver in her hand. "Everything's fine. It's not your fault. This is all *my* fault. Things are moving faster than I expected." She stared out the window, and Bree followed her gaze to see the game warden carrying the now-full bag to the back of the truck. "I was too late last night. And I won't be again. *Never again*." Aunt Hedda sighed. "I'm going to be busy today and tomorrow. There's a meeting at the town hall tomorrow, and I have to get ready for it." She looked back at Bree. "Do you think you can stay out of trouble and keep yourself occupied until then?"

"Sure," Bree said. "Nora and I have lots of work to do for the festival."

Aunt Hedda nodded. "Good. I won't need to worry about you too much then."

"Aunt Hedda, I —" Bree started, then stopped. She wanted to say that she didn't understand. Not one bit. What had her aunt meant when she'd said she was "too late"? For what? Was she talking about the houseguests? Maybe she meant that she'd forgotten to leave one of them outside as a meal for whatever thing was eating them nightly. Or maybe her aunt didn't know what she talking about at all.

Bree swallowed down the questions itching to burst out of her. Even if she did push her aunt for an explanation, what if her aunt didn't have any? Then what? Her mom and dad were halfway around the world. Would they believe her if she told them Aunt Hedda was certifiable? Probably not. Especially when they knew she hadn't even wanted to come here in the first place. No, Bree was going to have to figure out what was really going on in Midnight Lake all on her own. And she was going to have to do it before anything else, or — gulp! — anyone else, died.

CHAPTER NINE

"I don't understand where he is," Bree said to Nora, glancing at her watch. "He said he'd meet us here at nine o'clock, and it's a quarter after already." She sat down next to Nora on the rocks below Quin's house, blowing out a sigh of frustration.

"Are you sure he said he wanted to help?" Nora asked. "He didn't seem too into the idea last week."

"Yes," Bree said. "When I called him yesterday, he was completely on board. He said he had all these paints and plywood in his grandpa's toolshed that we could use."

Nora shook her head and then stood up, turning toward the house. "Well, I'm not going to let him ditch us. My mom's already freaking because the festival's on Saturday and the decorations are nowhere near ready. She'll go bananas if we don't finish the photo props. So, let's go get him."

Bree followed Nora up the path to Quin's house, feeling strangely nervous at the idea of seeing him. It would be the first time they'd hung out since their day fishing on Friday, and Bree had been thinking about him more than she wanted to admit. When she'd called him on Sunday, he'd sounded so excited about working on this project that she'd wondered if any of his enthusiasm had to do with seeing her. They'd talked for over an hour on the phone, and afterward Bree hadn't been able to stop smiling. But that had been yesterday, and so far today, he was nowhere in sight.

Bree knocked on the door, expecting Quin, but it was his grandpa who answered.

"Good morning, ladies!" Arvid said brightly. "To what do I owe the pleasure of your company?"

Bree and Nora exchanged glances and giggled.

"We're here for Quin," Bree said. "He said he wanted to help with the decorations for the Midsummer's Eve Festival."

Arvid nodded. "He mentioned something about that yesterday." A slight look of confusion muddled his face. "I got a slow start this morning . . . this darn contraption doesn't help much," he muttered, giving his wheelchair a thump with his fist. "The house was so quiet; I thought Quin was up and out already." He swung the door wider and motioned the girls inside. "Make yourselves at home. I'll go check his room."

Bree and Nora stepped into the simply furnished family room and waited. After a few minutes, Arvid came rolling back down the hallway with a rumpled, yawning Quin in tow.

"The lazybones was still dead asleep." Arvid grinned and tried to rough Quin's hair, but Quin ducked out from under his hand grouchily. "I don't know what's gotten into you lately, boy, wasting daylight. You're turning into a regular slug."

"Yeah, Quin," Nora teased, "what are you trying to do, stick us with all the work?"

Bree was about to laugh along with Nora and Arvid, but she could see by Quin's frown that he didn't think the razzing was all that funny. In fact, he looked more than tired; he looked . . . used up. His face had a gray chalkiness to it, and there were dark hollows carved out under his eyes.

"Sorry," he mumbled, running a hand through his wild hair. "I haven't been sleeping too great lately. I guess it's catching up with me."

"No problem," Bree said, waiting for some sort of sign from him that he'd actually noticed she was even in the room. But he barely looked at any of them.

"Nora, I heard what happened to Kari at the picnic," he said, keeping his eyes on the ground. "Is she all right?"

"She's fine. More of a pest now than ever." She rolled her eyes. "She's telling everyone in town that she got bit by the Midnight Lake Monster." Nora laughed. "She even drew all over her leg with red marker because she thought it would look like blood. Ridiculous."

"I'm sorry she got hurt," Quin said quietly.

"*She's* not." Nora shrugged. "Now she has something to brag about for the rest of the summer."

"Hey, do you feel okay, kiddo?" Arvid asked, peering at Quin with worried eyes. "You look a little . . . pale."

A little zombiefied was more like it, but Bree didn't say so. Instead, she said, "If you want to eat breakfast first, we can wait."

"No," Quin said quickly. "My stomach's kind of off." He shrugged, smiled wearily, and headed for the front door. "The paints and stuff are in the toolshed. Let's go."

Arvid waved them out the door, telling them he'd be in his workshop if they needed anything, and Quin led the way around the back of the house to the shed, where there were at least a dozen cans of paint and two large pieces of plywood.

"Grandpa already trimmed the edges and cut out the holes for people's heads to show through," Quin said. "The rest is up to us."

"These are great," Bree said, her mind already filling with possibilities for backgrounds and figures she could paint. Quin started prying open paint cans to reveal a variety of blues, greens, and browns. "Maybe we could do one with a mermaid and a fisherman on it."

"Ooh, I know!" Nora cried. "Let's do one with the body of the Midnight Lake Monster, or a swamp creature or something. Everyone will think that's hilarious!"

"Yeah," Bree said, liking the idea. "We could make it look totally silly. I could even paint it carrying Kari over its shoulder or something."

She waited for Quin to chime in, but he was laying tarps out on the grass in front of the shed, his brow furrowed miserably. She remembered how angry he'd gotten when Kari had brought up his great-uncle's drowning, and suddenly she realized that making light of that story might not be such a good idea after all.

"You know what?" Bree said. "I can't really draw monsters, so let's just stick with mermaids."

Nora started to protest, but Quin caught Bree's eyes and gave a small smile. Bree could see the relief in his face, and she knew she'd made the right choice.

They worked on the photo backdrops all morning, and Bree really gave in to her creativity, painting an underwater scene in the mermaid photo that she knew was some of the best art she'd ever made. Nora chattered happily the entire time, and thank goodness, too, because it made Quin's silence less awkward. He tried to joke around a few times, but Bree could see that it drained him to do it. He did tell her that her painting was terrific, which made her blush madly, but that was just about the only thing he said the entire time. She kept waiting for the real Quin to break through the weariness that strained his face, but it never happened. When they were all finished with the painting, Quin seemed relieved that it was over and that Bree and Nora were leaving.

"So," Bree said when they'd finished cleaning up, "thanks for letting us use all this stuff."

"No problem," Quin said. "Grandpa was glad to help out."

"Are you guys going to the town meeting tonight?" Bree asked hopefully. "Aunt Hedda's making me go, but at least if you're there I'll have someone to talk to."

"No way," Nora said, grimacing. "It's such a total snoozefest that I don't even care that my mom's making me babysit Kari while she goes."

Quin shook his head. "Grandpa's going, but I'm staying home. I need to practice my fiddle for the festival. I'm supposed to play with the band."

"Really?" Bree brightened. "That's amazing. Although I seriously doubt you need to practice. You sounded perfect when I heard you the other day."

"Thanks, but I can always be better, and Midsummer's Eve is only five days away." He sighed, and Bree thought a flicker of sadness crossed his face. "I'm running out of time."

"Then I guess I'll see you later," Bree said, feeling a sinking disappointment.

"Later," Quin murmured, already turning away to go inside.

"What's up with him?" Nora whispered to Bree as they walked away. "He's acting totally bizarre."

"Maybe he's getting sick or something," Bree said, hoping that that could explain why he was basically blowing her off after the fun time they'd had together on Friday. But somehow, that explanation didn't quite fit. Even after she said good-bye to Nora and went back to the beach to sketch and catch up on her reading, Bree couldn't stop thinking about Quin and how much he'd changed. And *change*, she realized, was the best word to describe it. Because something was definitely happening to Quin, and whatever it was was awful.

Bree stifled a yawn and sat up straighter in the folding chair, aware that her aunt was keeping tabs on her out of the corner of her eye. She was trying her best to at least look interested in the endless ramblings and complaints of the people speaking at the Town Hall meeting, but her mind kept drifting. Nora had been right, the meeting was a complete and utter bore.

During the few minutes before the meeting had started, Aunt Hedda had shuffled Bree around the large room, introducing her to half a dozen people in town she hadn't met yet. Bree had been pleased that her aunt spoke highly of her in the third person, calling her "bright" and "talented," things she would never have actually said to Bree herself. But now the meeting was under way, and it was all motions and "yeas" and "nays" and parking ordinances . . . sigh. Just as she was slipping away into another daydream about online shopping, she heard her aunt's name announced. The next thing Bree knew, Aunt Hedda was headed for the podium. Bree's heart quickened with dread. What was her aunt doing?

"Good evening, friends," Hedda said. "As you know, I requested this meeting in order to discuss the Midsummer's Eve Festival this coming Saturday."

Nods flew around the room, and Bree stiffened. Her aunt had *requested* the meeting? That was news to her.

"I know Midsummer's Eve is an important part of our heritage and our town's traditions," Aunt Hedda continued, "but I'm here to ask that we cancel the festivities this year."

Murmurs of protest rose up from dozens of people, and her aunt held up a hand for silence. "I know it will be a great disappointment to everyone, but conditions on the lake this year just aren't safe for our town."

"What do you mean?" one woman piped up. "There hasn't been an accident on this lake in fifty years."

"Exactly." Aunt Hedda nodded. "But I believe there might be a predator using the lake as a hunting ground this year. It's been killing animals, and it *will* kill people, just like it did before." Her piercing blue eyes seared the room. "I've seen creatures in this town most of you only see in nightmares. And I know it would be pure idiocy to let your children near the lake on Midsummer's Eve."

Bree's face burned, and she wished she could melt into the floor. It was one thing for her aunt to be eccentric in the privacy of her own home, but did she really have to flaunt it in front of the entire town?

"Come on, Hedda!" one man guffawed. "This sounds like another one of your quirky superstitions. We all know what you *think* happened to those kids who drowned years ago. But you can't keep the rest of us from having a good time."

"Think of how disappointed all the children will be if we cancel the celebration," Anna said.

Whispers broke out from others, and soon more people were chiming in, arguing to keep the festival going. Finally, Mayor Ericson eased up next to her aunt at the podium and called everyone to order.

"I'm sorry, Hedda," he said. "But I don't even see a need to put this to a vote. Everyone seems in favor of keeping the festival, so we're going to move on to the next piece of business."

Aunt Hedda's fist slammed into the podium, making it rattle deafeningly into her microphone. "Fine! Have it your way! But when tragedy strikes, remember that I warned you all." She stomped down the stairs from the podium and marched straight to the exit.

Bree scrambled out of her chair and followed her aunt through the doors and onto Main Street. The cool, misty night air relieved her fiery cheeks, but it didn't do much for the rest of her, which was dying from embarrassment. Aunt Hedda raged as she tore down the street toward home, ignoring Bree to the point that she wondered if her aunt remembered she was there at all.

"Fools," her aunt said. "They'll be sorry."

Bree was about to ask what she meant when a voice called out behind them. She turned to see Arvid Stromhest, wheeling furiously down the street.

"Hedda!" Arvid pulled the wheelchair right in front of her aunt, forcing her to stop. He was out of breath, but his eyes were sterner than Bree had ever seen them. "What was that all about back there?"

Aunt Hedda shook her head. "None of your concern," she snapped. She tried to turn away, but he blocked her again.

"You know it's my concern," he hissed roughly. He studied her face under the one lone streetlamp. Then he sighed.

"Quin's been disappearing at night," he said, frustration creasing his forehead. "Last night he didn't come home till dawn." He leaned toward Hedda, his eyes pleading. "What's happening? If Quin has any part in it, I'll —"

"He doesn't. I swear it." Her aunt said it with finality, keeping her eyes focused steadily on his. Then she straightened. "Let us pass, Arvid. Good night."

Arvid sighed again, then reluctantly backed away, letting them walk by. Bree looked over her shoulder once to see him slowly making his way back down the street, his head bent low.

"Aunt Hedda," Bree said softly, not wanting to set her aunt off again. "Do you really think there's something dangerous out there?"

"I know it," Aunt Hedda said. "And I'll tell you something else. Everyone else can risk their lives. But I have a duty to your mother and father, and *you're* not going to have any part of the Midsummer's Eve Festival."

Bree stopped mid-step, gaping at her aunt. "But I want to go," she said. "I've been helping with the decorations and —"

"Absolutely not," her aunt said. "And from now on, you're to be indoors by sunset every day, no exceptions."

"Sunset!" Bree cried. This was too much. She hadn't even done anything wrong! "My curfew at home isn't until ten, and that's in New York City! You're being completely unfair!"

"No," her aunt said firmly. "I'm doing what's best for you."

Bree stared at her, all of the pent-up frustrations she'd felt since she'd come to the lake suddenly boiling over. "You don't care what's best for me!" she erupted. "You don't even *like* me! You hate that I'm from the city and don't have 'practical' clothes or shoes, and you get annoyed that I don't like fish three meals a day. Ever since I came here, you've treated me like a clueless, spoiled brat. You talk about all the amazing things my dad used to do around here, and treat me like I'm a colossal waste of your time!"

Aunt Hedda's eyebrow shot skyward. "I never said that. . . ."

"But that's how you treat me!" Bree yelled. "You shut me out of everything, like whatever you're doing with your freaky pets on the back porch, and whatever happened with Quin that morning. Either you don't trust me at all, or you really are crazy like everyone thinks." She spat the last words out, and then clamped her mouth shut when she saw her aunt's stricken face, not believing she'd actually said them out loud. She sighed, her lip quivering. "All I want to do is get out of here and go back to New York where at least *somebody* loves me."

"Well," her aunt said slowly with a sad, haunted look in her eyes. "You can't. And for right now, you're under my roof and must obey my rules, and that's that."

"I wish I'd never come here!" Bree screamed. Tears stung her eyes, but she wasn't about to let Hedda see her cry. The lights of the house shone in the distance, and Bree pulled away from her aunt, breaking into a run. She took the stairs two at a time, tore through the house to her bedroom, slammed the door, and collapsed on her bed, giving in to racking sobs.

A few minutes later, she heard her aunt's footsteps come down the hallway and pause outside her door. But much to her relief, no knock came. Instead, the footsteps faded away, and Bree was left alone with her tears. Soon, her night music started, but tonight she couldn't find any comfort in its beauty. For the first time, she wished it would stop. Before tonight, Bree had just felt out of place in Midnight Lake. Now, she was beginning to feel like its captive. Or worse, like some sort of prey, although for what, or whom, she didn't know. But suddenly, more than anything, she just wanted to escape this town with its haunting music, mysteries, and darkness.

CHAPTER TEN

Bree had hoped that giving her aunt the cold shoulder might make her feel guilty enough for a change of heart. But as it turned out, aunts were just as immune to the silent treatment as parents. Bree stayed in her room most of Tuesday morning, watching movies on her iPad and whispering to Nora on her aunt's portable phone about being held hostage. When hunger got the best of her, she'd finally ventured into the kitchen, where she found a sandwich and some cookies waiting for her. Aunt Hedda was waiting for her, too, and for the rest of the day, she didn't seem to want to leave Bree's side. When Bree read on the couch, Aunt Hedda was there. When Bree went down to the lake to sketch and swim, Aunt Hedda set up a chair and umbrella on the beach.

So, when dinnertime rolled around and Aunt Hedda announced that she needed to go out for a few hours, Bree felt a wave of relief. Hopefully, her aunt would be gone long enough for Bree to do what she had to do.

"I have to go to the hardware store for a few things," her aunt told Bree. "It's outside town, but I won't be too far away. And I expect you to remember the rules." She pointed out the window toward the setting sun. "You'll stay inside now that dusk is falling."

Bree had to bite her tongue to keep from arguing. But the second her aunt's truck drove out of sight, she made a grab for the phone in the kitchen and quickly dialed her mom's international cell.

"Hedda, is that you?" Her mom's sleepy voice came over the line. "What's wrong?"

"No, Mom. It's me," Bree said. "I'm sorry I woke you. But I had to call." She sighed, and she tried to keep her voice from quivering. "Mom, I can't stay here anymore. Please."

"What?" Her mother's voice rose a notch. "Tell me what's going on."

So Bree told her everything about the house-guests, the bones on the beach, her aunt's ravings at the town meeting. And when she'd finished, she waited for her mom to shriek with horror and declare that Bree would be on the first plane to London.

But instead, her mom said, "Now, Bree, I don't want you giving your aunt a hard time. She has her strange notions and habits, but I know she has your best interests at heart. And I know she must have a good reason for keeping you from the Midsummer's Eve Festival."

Bree gripped the phone in a stranglehold, not believing what she was hearing. "But, Mom —"

"No 'buts,'" her mom said. "I know you can find a bright side to living in Midnight Lake. I'd hoped you would have found it already, but, well, there's still plenty of time." There was an audible yawn from her mom's end of the line. "Sweetie, it's four in the morning here, and your dad and I have a meeting with a rare-manuscript curator at eight. I have to go now."

"Fine, Mom, go," Bree said. Then, she added for dramatic effect, "But if you leave me here, this may be the last time you ever speak to me."

"I'll take my chances," her mom said. "Call if there's a real emergency. I love you."

"I love you, too," Bree said through clenched teeth. She hung up and dropped her head into her hands, wondering why parents never believe their kids about important things like, oh, say, crazy aunts and dead bodies.

She dragged herself to the sink to do the dishes, and finished the last one just as the sky began to get dark. She was about to watch another movie on her iPad when there was a knock on the screen door, and she saw Nora and Quin peeking through, grinning.

"We've come to rescue you from the wicked witch before she tosses you into the oven," Quin said as they stepped inside.

"I still cannot *believe* she's not letting you come to the festival," Nora said. "She's acting absolutely medieval. This is why living in this town terrifies me. It's like a black hole from which no modern thinking emerges. Your aunt's lived here her whole life, and look what's happened to her."

"I know." Bree giggled. "I'm really starting to think she's gone off the deep end. I got so sick of her breathing down my neck all day. But . . . she's not here right now."

Nora clapped. "Even better! We were going to hang with you inside, but now we can have some *real* fun." She grinned, and her eyes widened. "How about

I take you to see the ghost trees?" she asked, then cackled spookily.

"The what?" Bree looked at Quin, and he shrugged. But he was smiling, and Bree was relieved to see him looking much better than the last time she'd seen him.

"You'll see," Nora said, grabbing her hand to drag her to the door. "Come on."

Bree was dying to get out of the house, but still, she hesitated. "I don't know, guys," she said. "I'm not supposed to leave."

"We know." Nora rolled her eyes. "But we'll be back before Hedda is. And what your crazy aunt doesn't know won't hurt her, right?"

Bree giggled. "Okay. Let me get my shoes."

"I can't see a thing," Bree said as she tiptoed through the darkness, twigs and leaves crunching under her feet. "We should've brought flashlights."

"You can't see faerie fire with flashlights," Nora said mysteriously. "You have to be in complete and total darkness."

"Well, that's not a problem, is it?" Quin said teasingly from her left.

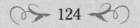

Bree giggled, but she couldn't stop the shiver that ran through her. When they'd walked into the woods from the lake, the sky had still been tinged gray with the last light of day. But once they were under the canopy of hemlock trees, the darkness grew, and now only scanty patches of light were showing here and there on the forest floor.

"You know, you're not too bad at hiking," Quin said to her as they stepped over a fallen tree trunk.

"Are you kidding me?" Bree said. "Have you ever walked around Manhattan? There are huge subway grates, sidewalk cellar doors, manholes. A girl has to be quick on her feet."

He laughed, and she smiled at him.

"I'm glad you're better today," she said suddenly and without thinking, then flushed. "I mean . . . you seem like you're more yourself now than when I saw you yesterday."

"I almost didn't come with Nora," Quin said. "But I do feel good today, so maybe it will be all right."

Bree wondered what he meant by that and was about to ask, but then Nora called out.

"It should be around here," she said, her voice coming from somewhere up ahead of Bree. "You'll know it when you see it. It's completely paranormal."

"I don't see anything," Bree started, but then she did. There was a faint, ghoulishly green glow up ahead through the trees. It was eerie, but also strangely lovely, too. "Omigod. What *is* that?"

She could see Nora smiling in the faint light, motioning her and Quin closer. "It's a special kind of fungus that glows in the dark. It's called *armillaria mellea*. It grows on rotting tree trunks. You can't even see most of it because it's underground and inside the tree. Before scientists found out what it was, people around here used to the think the woods were haunted."

"That's so cool," Bree said. "Quin, do you see it?"

Bree looked to her left, but he wasn't where he'd been just a minute ago. "Quin?"

A low moan behind her made her turn around, and there was Quin, kneeling on the ground, hunched over in pain.

"Are you okay?" Bree asked, bending over him. "Are you hurt?"

Quin shook his head, but she could see sweat trickling down his face, which was tinged green by the faerie-fire light. "I — I shouldn't have come," he panted. "I made a . . . terrible mistake."

"What do you mean?" Bree said. She reached an arm out to help him up, but he staggered to his feet and began running through the trees, away from her.

"Quin!" she called, taking off after him. "Wait!"

She tried to keep up with him, but he was running impossibly fast, deftly dodging trees and fallen logs as if he could see everything around him perfectly clearly. Bree could hear Nora calling behind her, but she kept running, only caring about helping Quin.

Finally, with her lungs aflame, she burst through the tree line onto the open beach just in time to see a shadowy figure she thought was Quin jump off the dock into the lake. She didn't hesitate. She could see that the water had already gone quiet, but she raced onto the dock anyway, hoping she'd see him somewhere. Her right foot hit the last plank and slid out from under her, and she fell backward, her head slamming into something hard and unyielding. A searing pain flashed across her skull, and a blaze of white fireworks exploded before her eyes. Then she plunged into the water. A sudden, lovely coolness wrapped itself around her, and soon she was floating, so peacefully.

She knew there was something she ought to be doing, but though her head was throbbing and she couldn't seem to take a breath, it wasn't entirely unpleasant, because she felt weightless and free, and so, so sleepy.

A glimmer of movement in the water ahead of her caught her eye, and then something sleek and nearly translucent shot toward her with lightning speed. There was a flash of bubbles, a flicker of weblike claws, and a split-second glimpse of shimmering liquid-silver eyes. An instant later, the creature snatched Bree around the waist and in one swift movement, propelled her out of the water and onto shore. Bree sucked in a hungry gulp of air, and then a murky veil slipped over her, drawing her into sleep.

A dull, heavy ache pounded Bree's eyelids, and when she forced them open, blinding needles of light pierced them. She clenched them shut, a groan escaping her lips, and then tentatively tried again. This time, her eyes opened onto the walls of her bedroom, which immediately began spinning.

She sat up slowly, and her room came into sharper focus. Her rumpled sheets, her dresser, her aunt asleep in a chair by the window. Wait a sec. *Her aunt was asleep in a chair by her window?* Bree gingerly touched the back of her head and felt a tender, mushrooming knot. She slid her feet over the side of the bed and stood up, but in an instant, overpowering dizziness dropped her back onto the bed with a loud thump.

Aunt Hedda's eyes flew open, and she was up out of the chair and at Bree's side in less than a nanosecond. "Get back into bed right now, missy!" she commanded roughly, but her hands were all tenderness as she tucked the covers back in around Bree. She sighed, surveying Bree with clear disapproval. "*You* have a concussion."

"What happened?" Bree said meekly, afraid she was in for the lecture of a lifetime.

But instead, her aunt sat down next to her on the bed and gave her hand an awkward, but well-intentioned pat. "You fell off the dock last night and whacked your head pretty good on one of the pilings. Nora saw you go in the water and ran for help, but then she heard a splash and a cough, and there you were on the beach. She called for me, and between the two of us, we got you back to the house. The nearest I can figure, you must have swum to shore before you lost consciousness. And a good thing, too." She offered Bree a scolding smile. "Imagine how unhappy your parents would've been if I'd told them that you disobeyed me *and* got yourself killed doing it."

"I'm sorry," Bree said hoarsely.

"I am, too," her aunt said gruffly. "I've been tough on you while you've been here, but . . . I'm tough on everyone." She leaned forward and whispered, "It doesn't mean I don't love you. Or that I think you're a spoiled brat. I actually think you've got a pretty strong head on your shoulders, *when* you're not trying to crack it open."

"Did you talk to Mom and Dad?" Bree asked. "Are they mad?"

"Your mom's called no less than ten times already this morning. And yes, of course they're mad, and so am I. But we're fairly convinced you've learned your lesson." She narrowed her eyes in a way that was both playful and threatening. "Have you?"

Bree started to laugh, then winced. "Yes." Her aunt didn't seem nearly as mad as she'd expected, which was a huge relief.

"Good. That's settled then." Her aunt stood up. "The doctor was here last night, but you probably don't remember. He said you're to stay in bed this morning. So I'll go make you some mint tea while you rest."

"Thanks," Bree said, sinking back onto her pillow with a sigh. She must've dozed for a minute or two, because when she opened her eyes again, it wasn't her aunt sitting by her bed, but Quin, holding a huge bouquet of wildflowers.

"Hey," he said quietly. "Your aunt told me what happened." He stared at the floorboards. "I'm so sorry. If I hadn't bolted out of the woods, then you wouldn't have come looking for me and this never would've happened."

"It's not your fault," Bree said. "It was just an accident. I thought I saw you jump into the water, so I followed you out on the dock."

He shook his head. "I — I didn't go in the lake. I went home. I . . . wasn't feeling well." He turned to look outside the window, avoiding her eyes. "It might've been something I ate."

Bree didn't believe him. Not one bit. He *had* gone into that water last night . . . she was sure of it.

"Anyway, it doesn't matter," Quin said, turning from the window to reach for something beside the chair. It was his fiddle. He picked it up and tucked it under his chin. "I thought I could play for you awhile, if you want. It might help you sleep."

Bree smiled. "I'd like that," she said, lying back again. "My head is killing me."

"Close your eyes," Quin whispered. He pulled the bow smoothly across the strings, and immediately Bree's headache lessened. She smiled as the music washed over her, and soon she was drifting off into a soft, sweet dreamland. But then she heard a subtle shift in the melody that changed everything. Now the music was filled with haunting notes that enchanted her, enthralled her. It was *her* night music, and *Quin* was playing it.

Her eyes flew open, and Quin's bow screeched to a halt.

"What song was that?" she asked, barely able to breathe.

"I — I don't know. Just some lullaby, I guess." He sprang to his feet, knocking his bow to the floor. He scooped it up and turned to the door. "I need to go. You need to rest, and I've got —" He shook his head as if he was trying to erase something awful from it. "There's something wrong with me. I shouldn't be around you. It's not good for you."

"Wait. Don't go," Bree said, struggling to sit up. "I don't understand . . ."

"It's better that way." He sighed. "Don't come looking for me. And don't come to my grandpa's. I won't let you in."

"But . . . why?" Bree said, an unexpectedly sharp sadness tearing through her.

Quin stopped in the doorway. "I'm sorry," he said.

He lifted his eyes to her face, looking at her for the first time since he'd arrived. A memory flared through the fog in her head, and she gasped.

"Your eyes," she whispered too late. Quin had gone.

CHAPTER ELEVEN

Bree dipped her brush into a blob of brick-red paint, then carefully touched its tip to the plate, swirling the paint into a flower bud.

"Very good," Aunt Hedda said, nodding in approval. "You're catching on to this so quickly. Why didn't I teach you *rosemåling* before?"

"Um, because I didn't have a concussion before?" Bree teased.

Her aunt laughed, sounding like a donkey with laryngitis. Bree was still getting used to that. The first time she heard it was yesterday afternoon, when Hedda had finally let her out of bed to help her make some *krumkaka*, a special Norwegian cookie shaped sort of like an ice-cream cone. Bree had accidentally dumped a bag of flour all over her shirt, and Aunt

Hedda had laughed so hard she got the hiccups. Suddenly, they were *both* laughing and — Bree could hardly believe it — having fun.

Then this morning when she'd woken up, Bree had found the kitchen table all set up with paints, brushes, and white ceramic plates.

"Since you're still a little wobbly on your feet," her aunt had said, "I thought we'd do something crafty." She pointed to the red-and-blue plates that hung on the wall of the living room. "It's a decorative Norwegian folk art called *rosemåling*. Do you want to try it?"

Bree did more than try it. She loved it. The colors, the brushstrokes, everything about it was wonderful. And even better was the patience her aunt showed teaching it to her. She didn't know if it was because she'd gotten hurt, or if she'd just finally given her aunt the chance she'd never given her before. Regardless of the reason, Bree had discovered that much of Hedda's hard exterior was for show. Oh, she was still tough, but it was tempered with a warmth toward Bree that hadn't been there before.

"There," Bree said as she added one final swirl to her plate and held it up. "What do you think?"

Aunt Hedda smiled. "You're going to have a nice collection to take back home with you at the end of the summer."

Bree put down her brush and stretched, sensing that now was the time to take advantage of her aunt's good mood. She had something she needed to do, and she'd been waiting until the timing was just right. "You know, I'm feeling a *lot* better now," she started. "I've been resting like I was supposed to, and the doctor said that walking was okay, and Nora's dying to see me. . . ."

Aunt Hedda snickered, shaking her head and waving a hand toward the door. "All right, all right, go ahead. Leave me here with my silly old paints."

"Thank you!" Bree said, jumping up. She planted a quick kiss on her aunt's cheek, pleased to see the look of delight and surprise it left on her face. "And your paints aren't silly. I like them, and I'm glad you showed them to me. I promise to paint more later." In the doorway, she turned back again. "And I promise to be home by sunset."

"Good," her aunt said. "Now go before I change my mind."

Bree scooted out the door, making sure she walked slowly down the path while she knew her aunt was watching. But as soon as the house was out of sight, Bree picked up the pace. She thought she'd done a pretty good job of pretending as if she'd forgotten everything that had happened when she'd hit her head on the dock. But ever since she saw Quin yesterday morning, it was his eyes that filled her thoughts. They were identical to the eyes of the creature she'd seen in the lake. She was sure of it, and now she was going to find out why.

When Bree walked into Anna's Bookstop, she was pleased to see that she was the only customer. That meant no nosy townsfolk listening to what she was about to tell Anna.

"Hi, Bree," Anna said from behind the coffee counter. "I'm so glad to see you're up and about! You gave us all a scare." She smiled. "Nora's in the back doing a puzzle with Kari. I can get her. . . ."

"Actually," Bree started, her heart fluttering nervously, "I need to do a little research first. I have to do some back-to-school reading on water creatures."

"Sure," Anna said, coming around the counter to thumb through the stacks of books. "We've got books on whales, manatees, dolphins. . . ."

"No." Bree swallowed thickly. Here went nothing. "I mean . . . unusual water creatures. Like mermaids, sort of, except different." She took a deep breath, and then slowly described everything she could remember about the creature she'd seen in the water. Of course, she didn't say she'd actually seen it. That would've just gotten her sent straight back to the doctor again. But as she described it as nonchalantly as she could, Anna's face lit up, and she snapped her fingers in triumph.

"It sounds like you're talking about the *nøkken*," she said. "One of my favorite scary stories from the old country."

"*Nøkken*?" Bree repeated. "What is it?"

"He's a shapeshifter," she said, moving to another bookcase. "A sort of water sprite. But he can take on lots of different forms. A human, lily pads, or a horrifying water monster." She pulled several books off the shelves and handed them to Bree. Then she sat down and opened one, showing Bree a picture of a hideous goblinlike creature with fangs, covered in green slime. "Here's one interpretation of what a nøkken might look like."

"No, that's not it," Bree said, then caught herself and added, "I mean, wow, that's ugly."

"That's the idea." Anna laughed. "The legend says that ages ago in Norway, a mermaid named Ona fell in love with a simple fisherman, Anders. The god of the ocean, Aegir, had sent Ona to lure Anders to his death on the rocks with her siren song. But Ona couldn't kill the fisherman. She fell in love with Anders, and he with her.

"Aegir saw all of this take place, and after listening to Ona's pleas, allowed the couple to wed as long as they promised never to return to the water again. He turned Ona from mermaid to woman so the couple could live together on land. But Aegir warned them about one thing. They were never to have a child together, for the child would be a cursed, monstrous creature, belonging to neither land nor water.

"The fisherman wanted to heed Aegir's warnings, but Ona wouldn't listen. She pined for a child of her own, and because Anders couldn't bear to see her unhappy, he finally agreed. Soon, a baby was born, and both parents were relieved to see that the baby seemed to be a normal human boy. The boy grew up healthy and strong, with his mother's gift of music and his father's talent for fishing. But as he neared his thirteenth birthday, he began to crave a life in the water, without understanding why. And one night, in a fit of madness, he dove into a deep lake, transforming into a strange water creature with unnatural cravings for blood.

"He longed to stay in the water, but he could not, because then he would be lost to his parents forever. So he shifted back and forth from human to beast, a lonely creature who never felt fully at home on land or in the water. The nøkken's only relief came from his music, which he supposedly played for his victims just before he dragged them into the water to their deaths."

"How awful." Bree sank back in her chair. "What a sad story."

"You think so?" Anna said, sounding surprised. "I always thought it was more scary than sad." A timer sounded from behind the counter, and Anna jumped to her feet. "That means my muffins are done. I've got to put some fresh ones out." She headed toward the back of the store. "Take your time looking through the books. You can check out any that you like. Just holler if you need me."

"Thanks," Bree said absently, already diving into the other books. She read every word about nøkkens that she could find, but that only made her spirits sink further and further. Every story told of a bloodthirsty beast beyond redemption. The last piece she came across was a short poem, and her skin crawled icily as she read:

In dismal, murky depths he waits,
Accursed by fickle fate,
Then rises up in darkest hour,
With hunger he can't sate.

With haunting song and woeful stare,
He lures you to his lair,
Take heed for it's your soul he craves,
A watery tomb, beware!

Bree shuddered, hugging herself to ward off a sudden chill. It couldn't be . . . could it? Though nøkkens were amazingly gifted musicians, like Quin. And Quin was an amazing fisherman *and* swimmer. Bree closed her eyes, feeling the truth hovering dangerously and wanting, more than anything, to escape it.

She was so caught up in her thoughts that when a cool hand clamped down on her shoulder, she jumped and gave a howl of fright.

"Whoa, there. Breathe," said Nora, leaning over her and laughing. "It's just me."

"I didn't hear you come over," Bree said.

"I guess not," Nora said, plopping down next to her on the oversize chair. "Mom told me you were here, so I thought you could help me pick out an outfit to wear to the festival. But you look busy." She nodded toward the smattering of open books. "What's with all the horror story stuff? And nøkkens?" She laughed. "My mom used to tell me stories about them before I could swim so I'd stay away from the lake."

"I don't know," Bree said, trying to sound as nonchalant as possible. She had to be careful here, because she didn't want to give too much away. "I thought I saw something weird in the water the other night when I hit my head. And, you know, with your sister getting bit and all . . ." She swallowed nervously, then blurted, "Maybe it's not such a bad idea to cancel the festival."

Nora stared at her. "You are *not* serious. You think we should cancel the whole thing because my sister got bit by some stupid eel or something?"

"All I'm saying is that maybe there is something . . . dangerous in the lake." Bree's pulse roared in her ears. She knew what she was going to say next would get a bad reaction. But she had to say it. "Maybe my aunt's right."

Nora raised her eyes to the ceiling. "You actually believe her crazy stories?" She snorted. "You know, I've spent my whole life around people who refuse to drive beyond a five-mile radius of this town. They shut themselves off from the rest of the world because they still think it's flat! I thought you were different. I don't get it. You don't even like your aunt! You complain about her all the time. And you said yourself that you thought she was insane."

"I'm sorry I said that." Bree shook her head. "I wasn't giving her a fair chance. It was before . . . before I knew —"

"Come on, Bree," Nora said, now serious. "The whole town knows she's losing her mind."

"She is not!" Bree said, standing up so quickly she knocked the books to the floor. "Hedda's been in this town longer than anyone else, and she knows things. . . ." Bree threw up her hands. "Just forget it. You talk about how close-minded this town is, and I admit that I thought so, too. But I was wrong, and so are you. But if you want to laugh at me, go ahead. I'm just sorry I said anything to you in the first place."

She walked to the door and flung it open. "I have to go. I'll see you later."

She closed the door in Nora's stunned face and turned toward home, her feet flying over the sidewalk, her mind floundering between belief and confusion, fury and embarrassment. She didn't know what the truth was, but she thought she knew who did. Her aunt wasn't home when she got there, so Bree grabbed her sketchbook and got to work. She worked on the drawing all afternoon, until she heard the truck pull into the driveway. Then she sat down with her sketchbook at the kitchen table, hoping she was ready for whatever answers were about to walk through the door.

Her aunt came in with a smile, proudly holding up a brown takeout bag. "I drove all the way to Crossbridge to get you dim sum," she said. "Your dad told me it was your favorite."

"Thanks," Bree said, feeling a pang of guilt that she was about to ruin her aunt's surprise dinner. She sucked in a breath, then plunged ahead before her courage deserted her. "I know what saved me that night in the lake," she said, sliding her sketchbook toward her aunt, watching her face closely. "A nøkken. And this is what he looked like."

Aunt Hedda paled, and the takeout bag slipped out of her arms and landed with a dull thud on the floor. She stared at Bree's drawing, her expression lost between fear and consternation.

Then she blinked, cleared her throat, and abruptly turned to pick up the dropped bag. "You're imagining things —"

"No," Bree said firmly. "I know what I saw." She held her aunt's eyes, refusing to give in. "It's Quin, isn't it?" she said quietly. "He's a nøkken."

A full minute passed and her aunt didn't move or speak, and Bree felt as if she was locked in a silent battle of wills. Then, finally, her aunt sighed wearily and sat down across from Bree. "Tell me everything you know," she said calmly.

And Bree did. Starting with the animal bones she found along the shore, she told her aunt everything, describing all of Quin's strange behavior and the stories she read at Anna's Bookstop. When she was finished, Aunt Hedda leaned back in her chair, studying her.

"You're quite the detective," she said finally. "And some of what you've read is true." She leaned forward, her keen eyes two icy orbs. "But . . . there's more."

Bree's stomach plunged. "What do you mean?"

"That first nøkken that Anna told you about," her aunt continued. "The son of Ona and Anders. He fell in love with a beautiful woman. So he left the water for a time, taking his human form so he could be with her." Her aunt sighed. "They had a family together."

"What?" Bree whispered.

"Yes," Aunt Hedda said. "But the nøkken couldn't stand to stay on land, even for his own children. Eventually, he returned to his watery home. But his children, and children's children, remained behind on land as humans." She shook her head. "Except for a few that inherited the curse."

In one staggering instant, the puzzle pieces in Bree's mind snapped into place. "Quin?" she whispered.

Aunt Hedda nodded sadly. "The Stromhests are descendants of the first nøkken. Some of them have been able to lead normal lives. But every fifty years, a single boy is born a nøkken." She frowned at the table, and Bree could tell she was struggling with what came next. "The transformation begins with the first blood moon and is completed by Midsummer's Eve."

Bree's breath caught in her throat, and she couldn't stop trembling. "But Midsummer's Eve is in two days. So when it comes, Quin will be . . ."

"A nøkken forever," Hedda finished for her. "He'll forget what it is to be human. He may still be able to assume human form, but his cravings and loneliness will overtake his human memories. After Midsummer's Eve, he'll be more beast than boy. The human part of him won't want to kill, but if the beast part gains total control, he won't be able to stop himself."

"So that's why you've been leaving him the animals by the lake!" Bree exclaimed, everything becoming clear.

"I was trying to teach him to control his cravings," she said, defeat in her voice. "To only take animals and not . . . humans. But Quin can't remember most of what happens when he's in his nøkken form." She sighed. "That's why I wanted to cancel the festival. I don't know what he'll do once his transformation is complete. I think he's in danger of losing the battle."

"No," Bree said. "He didn't hurt me that night I hit my head. He saved me." She ran her hand over the sketch she'd made of him. No matter what form he took, Quin's eyes were still the same: sharp, soulful, and undoubtedly human. "Isn't there any way to break the curse?"

"There is only one way that I know of, and it's complicated," Aunt Hedda said. "Every nøkken has one kindred soul that he seeks — someone who cares for him always, no matter what form he takes. First that person must willingly follow him into the water. Next they must make the nøkken remember his human form by saying his name three times. And then, if the nøkken is able to remember his own name, he will assume his human form again."

Bree's heart stopped. "But who is the nøkken's kindred soul?"

Aunt Hedda studied Bree for a long time, and Bree knew the answer before her aunt said it. "The person who hears his music in the night. The only person who *can* hear it."

"I've heard it," Bree whispered. "Every night since the blood moon."

"I know," Aunt Hedda said, giving Bree's hand a squeeze. "I acted like I didn't, but I knew. For you to break the curse, though, would be impossible."

"Why?" Bree asked. "I could at least try . . ."

"No," her aunt said with finality. "That wouldn't break the curse completely. Every year there would be another Midsummer's Eve. In order to free Quin forever, another Stromhest must volunteer to take the curse onto himself. And Quin has no family to do it."

"But, Arvid . . ."

"Never," Aunt Hedda said, her voice breaking harshly. "Arvid deserves to finish his life in peace. I've caused him enough heartache over the years. He knows nothing of what's happening to Quin, and it's going to stay that way."

"But why shouldn't he know?" Bree asked. "He might *want* to help him."

"I can't ask that of him again," Aunt Hedda said. "I did once before . . . fifty years ago." She pressed the palms of her hands into her eyelids, looking more tired than Bree had ever seen her. "Arvid's brother, Thomas, and I were . . . sweethearts. We'd known each other since we were babes, and loved each other just as long. We were so young, but we were dead set on marrying." Her voice wavered. "The curse came to Thomas late, at sixteen. That summer, when the blood moon came, he began to change, and I was the one who heard his music." She closed her eyes, caught up in the memories. "I went to Arvid and begged him to save Thomas, and he agreed. I didn't know it then, but Arvid was in love with me, too. It broke his heart to see me with Thomas, but he didn't want to see me heartbroken either. So he tried. We both did. But Thomas wouldn't let us save him. He loved his brother too much to let him take on the curse." She wiped at her eyes angrily. "On Midsummer's Eve, Thomas became a nøkken forever."

"I'm sorry," Bree whispered. "It must have been terrible for you, and for Arvid."

"It was a lifetime ago, but the pain still rears its head, even so. It was a tragedy," her aunt said matter-of-factly. "Thomas was a good man, but he couldn't control the beast he became. The nøkken killed that summer. And on the last night I saw him as a human, he found out what he'd done. After that, he refused to stay in a place where he could do harm. So, after Midsummer's Eve, he just . . . disappeared."

"How?" Bree asked.

Hedda walked over to the window and looked out at the glittering lake. "There are several forms the nøkken can take," she said. "A water beast. A human. And a horse."

"Stromhest," Bree said, remembering with lightning clarity. "Stream horse."

"Yes," her aunt said. "That night, I saw a beautiful white stallion gallop off into the forest. The drownings in the lake stopped, and I never saw Thomas again."

The kitchen was so quiet, the only thing Bree could hear was the faint ripple of the waves along the lake. She didn't know how long she and Aunt Hedda stayed like that, lost in thought, but finally, her aunt cleared her throat and turned from the window, breaking the spell.

"Well, here's the dim sum, if you want it." Her aunt set the bag down in front of Bree, then put her hand on Bree's shoulder, letting it rest there for a moment before pulling away. "I'm sorry that there's nothing we can do for Quin," she said wearily.

"But why couldn't Quin just turn into a horse?" Bree asked. "Like Thomas did?"

"A nøkken can only become a horse after his full transformation," her aunt said. "And by then, Quin might not have enough self-control to take the horse form. In order to change, he'd have to have enough willpower to overcome his thirst for blood. But he's younger than Thomas was, and his cravings are already very strong." She looked at Bree soberly. "I won't have you risk your life when it won't do any good in the end. The only thing we can really do now is try to keep everyone in town safe, whatever happens."

"But I know we can save him," Bree said. "There has to be a way."

"I wish there were." Her aunt kissed the top of her head, then blew out a long breath. "I'm going to bed. I have some important things to do before the festival." She started down the hallway, then turned back. "It would be best if you tried to accept the way things are."

"But then what?" Bree said, her eyes filling with tears.

Heartache shone in her aunt's eyes. "Then . . . you let Quin go."

CHAPTER TWELVE

Bree would never let Quin go. She knew it with the same certainty that she knew when sunlight made a day perfect for sketching, or when a flower was asking to be drawn. But for all of Friday and most of the day Saturday, she pretended that that was exactly what she was going to do. She didn't argue with her aunt about the festival anymore. Instead, she decided to be as helpful and agreeable as possible, so her aunt wouldn't suspect anything.

On Friday afternoon, she met Anna and a whole group of locals on the beach near the harbor to decorate for the festival. Aunt Hedda had at least agreed that she could help set up, even if she wouldn't be at the actual festival. So, for most of the afternoon, Bree kept her mind focused on making the garlands for the maypole and setting up the game and food booths. Nora was working, too, and although there was one awkward moment when they'd nearly bumped into each other carrying wood for the bonfire site, they stayed out of each other's way. And for the most part, Bree was glad. She wasn't much in the mood for talking, and clearly, neither was Nora. And even if Nora had apologized to her, Bree wasn't sure what she would've said in return.

So she finished up decorating with a heavy heart. She stopped by Arvid's house on the way home and knocked on the door, but there was no answer. The house had an uneasy quietness to it, and Bree sensed that Quin was inside, listening for her and watching.

She put her cheek up against the door. "Quin," she said. "I know you're in there. And I know you don't want to see me, but I'm leaving you something." She ripped the sketch that she'd worked on all that morning out of her notebook. It was a drawing of Quin, and she thought it was one of the best drawings she'd ever done. She'd tried to capture the mischief of his eyes, his carefree smile, everything about him that was infectious, fun, and oh-so-human.

Now, she slipped her pencil out from her sketch pad and scrawled across the bottom of the sketch: NEVER FORGET WHO YOU REALLY ARE.

She folded it and carefully slid it under the front door, and then went home and waited. Waited through another painful twenty-four hours of killing time, of pretending that she was dealing when she wasn't. She waited until Saturday afternoon, when the sun started to sink toward the mountaintops, and then she put her plan into action. Aunt Hedda had just put her dinner plate down in front of her when Bree gave a weak moan, closed her eyes, and gripped the edge of the table.

"Bree?" Aunt Hedda said. "What is it?"

"Nothing," Bree said, rubbing her forehead for dramatic effect. "I just felt a little dizzy for a second, but it's gone now."

Her aunt peered at her face. "You look pale. Are you sure you're all right?"

Bree nodded hesitantly, then sighed. "It's just . . . well, I've had a headache all day. I didn't want to tell you before. . . ."

"You should've told me right away," her aunt said. "That was one of the things the doctor said to watch out for after your concussion." She shook her head. "Why don't you go lie down for a while? I'll call the doctor."

"Okay," Bree said, moving as slowly down the hallway as she could, hoping she looked unsteady on her feet. Once inside her room, she shut the door, collapsed against it, and let out a whoosh of breath. Well, she'd fooled her aunt. Now all she had to do was get out of the house without breaking her neck.

She grabbed the long piece of rope she'd found earlier in the garage, opened her window wide, and looped the rope over the dragon's head outside her bedroom window. She knew she had to hurry before her aunt came into the room. So, not giving herself a chance for doubts, she swung herself out the window and, clinging to the rope, shimmied down the side of the house to the gravel drive below.

The second her feet hit the ground, she was running. The setting sun was already silhouetting the mountains in fiery red. And once night fell, her one and only chance would be over.

The dirt path along the water's edge was darkening with every passing second, and Bree could hear the distant music from the festival growing louder as she ran. She could make out the glow of the bonfire farther down the beach, but it would probably still take her at least a few more minutes to get there. Her breath came in harsh gasps, and her lungs burned, but she pushed herself to run faster. It wasn't until she was crashing into something blocking the path in front of the Stromhest house that she could catch her breath.

"Easy does it, girl," Arvid said. "Where are you racing off to in such a fury?"

"I'm sorry," Bree said frantically. She could see the outline of his wheelchair in the gray light, but she cursed herself for not seeing it before. He was the last person she wanted to see right now "I didn't see you there. But I'm in a hurry, and I really have to go. . . ."

"I know you do," Arvid said, and there was a certainty in his voice, as if he knew exactly where she was going, and why. "You're looking for Quin, too, aren't you?"

Panic surged through her. "No, I . . . I'm just heading to the Midsummer's Eve Festival." There was a nervous lilt to her voice that she was sure was giving her away. "I'm late."

"You don't have to lie." The knowing in Arvid's eyes was terrifying and reassuring all at once. "I didn't want to see it, but I did. I wanted so badly for Quin to be spared. You've seen the truth, just like I have."

Bree shook her head. "I don't know what you're talking about."

"Yes, you do." Arvid stared into her eyes, his own pained and desperate. "You see, I thought Quin had gone fishing this afternoon. He left me a note saying so, and the house was quiet. But a few minutes ago, I was sitting out on the porch watching the sunset, and I heard this screaming and pounding from our toolshed out back. Someone had locked it from the outside with a huge padlock and chains. I could hear my boy in there tearing at the walls." His voice broke. "I tried to get to him sooner, but this stupid chair stopped me. And then something — I think it was Quin, it *had* to be Quin — broke out of the shed and ran toward the lake."

He pointed to the small shed alongside the house, and even in the murky shadows of dusk, Bree could see a side of the shed had been torn clean away, leaving a jagged, gaping hole.

He grabbed Bree's hand, clenching it in his own. "You know what's happening to him, don't you?"

Bree knew if she looked at the sadness in Arvid's face for even a second longer, she'd break down and tell him everything. But there wasn't time. Quin was in the water, changing . . . forever. She wrenched her hand from him and staggered away. "I'm sorry," she called back, breaking into a run.

The few minutes it took her to reach the festival were sheer agony. She ran at a fever pitch, but with every second that passed, she wondered if she was already too late. The dirt path finally opened onto the wide stretch of beach along the town harbor, and Bree stumbled into the crowd. The festival was chaotic and loud, brimming with laughter and music. The bonfire was as tall as a house, sending showers of sparks high into the blackening sky, and children were splashing and swimming in the lake by the glow of its light. A band played a foot-stomping dance beat from the large wooden stage, and Bree could see a few people lined up to stick their heads into the plywood scenes she'd painted for photo ops.

"Isn't it a shame that we won't hear Quin on his fiddle tonight," she heard Anna telling Mayor Ericson.

"He was supposed to be up there with the band, but he called me this morning to say he was sick and wouldn't be able to come. I think it's the first time he's ever missed the festival."

Bree ducked away from Anna, her heart quickening at the mention of Quin's name. So he'd told everyone he was sick, and then he somehow locked himself into the shed to try to keep from hurting anyone. But it hadn't worked.

Bree skirted around the maypole with its colorful garlands, which stood in the center of a dozen game booths and food stands. She caught a glimpse of Nora and Kari dancing happily around it with a bunch of other kids, but she managed to avoid them. Running into someone she knew right now would only slow her down, and she didn't want anything getting in the way of what she had to do.

She hurried away from the warmth of the bonfire toward the pier, where she was a safe distance away from the crowds and could keep a sharp eye on the kids swimming and on the rest of the lake. Then she perched on the edge of the pier and waited.

It didn't take long. Just as the very first star blinked into the sky, she heard Quin's night music. Even above the rowdy band, it came to her, more inside her head than anywhere else. This time, she didn't fight it. This time, she gave in to it.

"I'm right here," she whispered, slipping into the water. "Come find me."

She saw a glimmer in the lake about a hundred feet from where the children were wading in the shallows, and she shot through the water after it, willing her body to move faster than she'd ever forced it to before. Just as he was about to swim within reach of a toddler, Bree blocked his path. He spun toward her, and in a fury of frothing water, he was upon her, latching on to her waist with inhuman strength.

She sucked in a huge breath of air and, in the distance, saw Aunt Hedda running toward the water, screaming, "No!" Then she was under, churning downward so rapidly that the passing water roared in her ears like thunder. He was behind her, his arms like a chain around her, and she knew if she didn't turn, if she couldn't show him her face, they'd both be lost. She wrestled to free herself, tearing at the sleek, glistening scales binding her, and finally, he loosened his grip just enough for her to spin around.

There was an unearthly beauty in his face, in the glittering kaleidoscope of sea greens and blues in his feathery fins. And his molten-silver eyes looked more frightened than wild, more sad than raging.

She strained against him, using her legs to propel both of them toward the surface, where she broke through, choking for air. "Quin!" she said, as his grip tightened. "Quin!" as he yanked her back. "Quin!" as her face dipped under again.

For a second, his eyes stayed locked on hers, unchanging. But then, suddenly, there was a softening, a spark of recognition. A tornado of bubbles and blinding light engulfed them, and Bree had to shut her eyes against it. But when she opened them again, it was on the still, smiling face she knew so well. Quin slipped his smooth, pink hand into hers and pulled her to the surface.

"I knew you'd remember," Bree said as they began swimming toward shore.

"I hoped you'd come," he said. But then, a second later, he gave a howl of pain and pulled away from her, hiding his face behind webbed hands.

"No," Bree said. "Stay." But he was changing again, back into the nøkken. And this time, there would be nothing Bree could do to bring him back.

"Let me go," Quin moaned in a voice that was

more animal than human. But Bree just wrapped her arms around him tighter.

She barely felt another pair of arms encircling her, prying her away. But then she was alone and shivering in the water, and Arvid was beside Quin.

"I couldn't save Thomas," Arvid said to him. "But I *will* save you."

"No," Quin said. "I won't let you."

"Give me the curse," Arvid commanded. "I've been a prisoner in this body for years." He reached out his hand toward Quin. "Set me free."

Quin shook his head and tried to pull away, but Arvid grabbed him by the arm, and forced his own hand into Quin's, fusing them together. There was another flash of blinding light, and then darkness settled over the water once more. Bree opened her eyes to find Quin in her arms, shivering and weak, but entirely human. And farther out in the lake, a sleek sapphire creature sluiced away through the water, swift and agile. Arvid had become the nøkken.

CHAPTER THIRTEEN

Bree woke up to sunshine pouring through her window and to the sound of music. It was a quiet song, with an undercurrent of gratefulness and sadness, like the kind of song you'd sing to honor someone lost. But even though Bree heard the grief, and understood it, she was still able to smile. Because this music wasn't haunted or hungry. It didn't call her away to dangerous waters, or consume her mind. It was simply . . . beautiful.

She got dressed and followed the music out of her bedroom and through her aunt's house. When she stepped onto the back porch, Quin looked up from his fiddle and smiled so broadly that a swift heat swept across Bree's cheeks. He looked tired, and there was a bandage on his arm from where

Bree had scratched him in their struggle in the water, but there was quickness in his eyes again and more color in his face than Bree had seen all week.

"Hey," he said, motioning for her to have a seat at the rickety card table her aunt had set with breakfast. "We saved you some pickled herring."

Bree grimaced, then laughed. "Please tell me you're kidding."

"Actually, we thought you might like a little taste of home," Aunt Hedda piped up. "I made a trip to the food mart early this morning and brought these back." With a theatrical bow that was completely out of character for her, she whipped a dish towel off a plate on the table to reveal a mound of golden-brown

"Bagels!" Bree cried, her mouth already watering.

"And lox, of course," her aunt said with a teasing wink. "It wouldn't be a proper Norwegian breakfast without *some* fish."

She patted the empty folding chair next to Quin's, and Bree gratefully took a seat. She grabbed a bagel and smeared it with mouthwatering cream cheese and chives, then took a huge, delectable bite. "Mmmm," she said between mouthfuls. "I never thought I could miss a piece of bread so much." She took another bite, and then glanced around the screened-in porch, for the first time noticing the vacant walls and floors. "Hey! The houseguests are gone!"

Aunt Hedda nodded. "We let them all go earlier this morning. We didn't need them anymore, did we?" She motioned to the lovely view of the lake beyond the porch. "I always wanted a breakfast nook out here." She smiled. "Now that I'm free of all those wretched creatures, I can have one."

The muffled ring of the telephone came from inside the house, and her aunt stood to get it. "You two eat up," she said. "I'll be back."

After the door had swung shut and the two of them were alone, Bree found herself staring at the tablecloth, her heart thrumming like a hummingbird's. So much had happened between her and Quin, and now she felt suddenly awkward and tongue-tied. But when she finally risked a glance at him, she saw him watching her, his eyes sparkling.

"I'm sorry about your grandpa," Bree said quietly.

Quin nodded, looking out at the lake. "Me too. But . . . I think it really was what he wanted." He pulled a piece of paper out of his pocket and handed it to Bree. "He left me this note."

Bree took it carefully, and read:

Quin,

By the time you read this, I'll be gone. I wished so many times in your life that I'd been able to give you more. To do more for you. Now's my chance. Don't be sad for me. I always hated that infernal chair.

Years ago, I made arrangements with Hedda for her to watch over you if anything ever happened to me. I know she'll be good to you and love you like her own kin. Never forget how proud I am of you and that I love you, always.

Grandpa

Bree handed the note back to Quin. "So he must have suspected something even before last night."

Quin nodded. "I think so. I tried so hard to keep it from him," he said. "That's why Hedda locked me in the shed yesterday afternoon. We were trying to keep everyone from getting hurt."

"So that's how you got locked in!" Bree cried. "I wondered how you'd managed that."

"It was *my* idea. I thought that maybe, if I couldn't get to the water, I might not change." He sighed. "It didn't work."

"So . . . you're going to stay with Hedda?" Bree asked, staring at her hands in her lap.

"At least for now," Quin said, and then he laughed. "You're going to be completely sick of me by the end of the summer."

"I don't think so," Bree blurted, then sucked in a breath of air. Oh my god . . . had she actually just said that out loud?

She blushed furiously and reached for her orange juice, but Quin caught her hand in his instead. Then he smiled, and she knew that, even though the curse was gone, she was still caught in his spell. And she knew, just like he said, that this was where she belonged. Maybe not for forever, but for the rest of the summer, which stretched out lazily and wonderfully in front of her.

"Thanks," Quin said, "for saving me last night."

"Well, you rescued me once, too," Bree said, grinning. "I figured the least I could do was return the favor." She elbowed him. "I still haven't forgiven you for my shoes, though."

"Whoa," a familiar voice said, and they glanced up to see Nora standing on the landing, staring at the two of them holding hands. "I must've missed something *huge* in the last two days."

"You have *no* idea," Quin said, making Bree giggle.

"And you have no idea what a total bore the festival was without you two there," Nora said. "Kari made me dance around the maypole with her at least a hundred times. Aside from this freak electrical storm that made lightning over the water, which was pretty cool, I was dying without you guys." She stared uncomfortably at the floor, then looked up at Bree.

"Can you please not be mad at me anymore?" she said to her. "If you and I don't start talking again, the rest of my summer is going to be positively stagnant. I'm sorry I said all those nasty things to you the other day. I mean, so what if you believe in mythical water creatures and weird folktales, right? My own mother still believes that little people live under our floorboards." She rolled her eyes. "Anyway, I don't care what you believe, I just want us to be okay again." She let out a big poof of air she'd been holding in, then added, "I need your fashion advice, sure, but I *want* your friendship."

Bree laughed and then hugged Nora. "Thanks for the apology. I missed you, too. But as far as fashion goes, I think it's time we start planning your first trip to New York for some in-depth experience. And you have to meet Fiona. She is a way more devoted fashionista than I am. Maybe you can come during spring break next year." She looked at Quin. "Maybe you both can."

Quin raised an eyebrow. "What are you saying — that I don't have good fashion sense?" Then he laughed. "Just kidding. I'd like that a lot."

"I can't wait to ask my mom." Nora squealed. "Omigod, I'll have to go shopping before the trip just to have something worthy to wear."

Bree laughed. "Oh, but I do want to set the record straight about one thing," she added to Nora. "You were right about the water creatures." She looked at Quin, and smiled. "They're just a figment of our imaginations."

The second the words left her mouth, she heard a loud rustling and crackling of branches from the edge of the woods, like something large was moving through the trees. All three of them turned to look, and there, beside the grove of hemlocks, was a beautiful white stallion grazing on the grass.

"Would you look at that," Hedda whispered as she stepped back onto the porch. "Isn't he a sight."

"He looks really . . . happy," Quin said.

The stallion raised his head and looked at them, tossing his mane as if he were nodding in agreement.

He whinnied, spun on his hooves, and galloped away, disappearing among the trees.

"I've never seen a wild horse at the lake before," Nora said. "I wonder what he was doing so close to people."

"Oh, just saying hello," Aunt Hedda said. "And . . . good-bye." She wrapped an arm around Quin, giving his shoulder a squeeze, and then smiled at Bree.

"Bree," she said. "That's your mother on the phone. We talked for a bit, and she wants to say hello to you."

Bree quickly went inside and picked up the phone.

"Hi, sweetie," her mom said. "I just wanted to check up on you. You sounded so homesick and upset the other night, and I was worried. Maybe it wasn't fair of us to ask you to spend the summer so far away from home." She sighed. "I know your aunt can be grouchy, and you miss your friends —"

"Mom," Bree interrupted. "It's fine, really. I'm not homesick anymore." She smiled as she heard Quin and Nora laughing with Aunt Hedda from the porch, and she was already itching to get back out there to join in. "I was actually thinking that I'd like to come back to Midnight Lake again next year. This is turning out to be the best summer vacation I've ever had. You might even say it's been . . . magical."

POISON APPLE BOOKS

The Dead End

This Totally Bites!

Miss Fortune

Now You See Me...

Midnight Howl

Her Evil Twin

Curiosity Killed the Cat

At First Bite

THRILLING.
BONE-CHILLING.
THESE BOOKS
HAVE BITE!